The Boy from An Giang

Vinh Quyen Tang

Nghĩa Lan Nhân

Recognition

(from the Vietnamese edition 'Đứa Con An Giang,' translated into English as 'The Boy From An Giang')

'Đứa Con An Giang' came into being through the direct or indirect contributions of many people. Although a work of fiction, it is based on real events, circumstances, and numerous anecdotes the author shared with fellow compatriots during a unique chapter in the nation's history.

My first words of gratitude go to the "brothers and sisters" who lived through those final months of 1975. Though some are still with us and others have passed, my wife and I deeply cherish the kindness you showed us and the many dear memories we shared together.

Even so, 'Đứa Con An Giang' could never have matured without the care and attention of its many other "aunts and uncles" - those who read the manuscript, offered words of encouragement, or took the time to help edit the book.

Here, my wife and I would like to extend our heartfelt thanks to Mr. Trần Lương Ngọc, who patiently corrected countless spelling errors - far too many! Mr. Ngọc also helped refine certain passages and generously contributed a moving piece, 'An Giang Cảm Đề', which we are honored to feature in his handwriting on the back cover.

Within the soul of 'Đứa Con An Giang', his verse echoes like a soft chime in a cavern, stirring droplets of water that suddenly glide down a stalactite and fall into a still pond, gently rippling a silence thought long forgotten.

I would also like to express my gratitude to another friend who once guided me in community work. Many know him as Dr. Lê Duy Cấn, a long-standing contributor to the Vietnamese community in Canada, who helped bring to life several lasting initiatives in the capital city of Ottawa.

Among these is his support for the construction of the first Vietnamese Boat People Memorial in Canada in 1995, featuring the 'Mother and Child' statue by sculptor Phạm Thế Trung. This monument holds profound meaning for our compatriots and has since become a landmark visited by many tourists to the capital.

Another equally significant project he is currently dedicating great effort to, alongside members of the community, is the Vietnamese Boat People Museum, which will be located across from the 'Mother and Child' Memorial.

For 'Đứa Con An Giang', Mr. Cẩn took the time to print out the manuscript, read it line by line, and helped correct spelling errors as well as offered thoughtful suggestions to improve the book. My wife and I will always hold this kindness in our hearts.

Having known Mr. Cẩn for many years, I deeply admire his gracious demeanor toward everyone, at all times, whether in someone's presence or absence. May his kind heart and genuine respect for others continue to illuminate the path of community service he has long chosen - a path he embarked upon back when he was still a high school student in Vietnam, continued through his student years in Canada, and has remained faithful to ever since.

Lastly, my wife and I would like to extend our sincere thanks to Architect John Le (Lê Trường Sơn), who generously devoted his valuable time to creating the unique and meaningful cover illustration that introduces Đứa Con An Giang in an exceptionally elegant and memorable way.

Tăng Quyền Vinh
Ottawa, 06-08-2022.

TABLE OF CONTENTS

Preface

"Đất An Giang phù sa màu mỡ,
Người An Giang muôn thuở hiền lành."

(Fertile is the alluvial land of An Giang,
And gentle are its people, now and forever.)

This folk song speaks the truth, and 'The Boy from An Giang' stands as living proof. His story reminds us that whether rooted in the heart of our homeland or scattered across distant shores, we continue to carry our homeland within us.

In the pages that follow, you'll journey into the life of the boy from An Giang - his origins, identity, path through life, and matters of the heart. Along the way, I hope you'll catch a glimpse of an entire refugee community in its earliest days in a new land, told through the lives, characters, struggles, and hopes of its people - those striving, against all odds, to begin life anew.

I invite you to listen to the old music carried in the soldier's backpack - cassette tapes brought from his homeland. In the voice of Hương Lan, you'll hear the bittersweet tenderness of endive; in Hà Thanh's singing, the deep tranquility of the ancient imperial capital; and through Phương Hồng Quế, the sincere affection of the girl next door.

These songs open a window into the hearts of the Vietnamese people in a faraway land - from the early days when they walked through

North American airports in worn-out sandals to their first 'Tết'
Festival abroad, and through every day that followed.

May these echoes of the past open the door to the future, and may
rays of hope continue to illuminate their historic journey.

I look forward to meeting you again within the pages of The Boy
from An Giang.

Preface Footnotes

*1. In this book, you'll find selected passages translated from the Vietnamese
edition of 'Đứa Con An Giang'. Where appropriate, additional context has
been included to help non-Vietnamese-speaking readers understand and
appreciate the material more fully.*

*2. Some characters are addressed by a number, such as Mr. or Mrs. Four,
Five, or Six. This reflects a Vietnamese tradition of referring to people by
their birth order within the family, plus one. For instance, the first child is
called Mr. or Mrs. Two, followed by Three, Four, and so on. Interestingly,
there is no Mr. or Mrs. One!*

*3. The translation and supplemental writing in this book were completed by
the author with significant assistance from ChatGPT.*

1. The Flashlight

Tuất was a Vietnamese-Canadian man in his late thirties, with a dark complexion and a tall, robust build that hinted at a life once lived closer to the equator. There was an air of quiet mindfulness about him, but it was his infectiously pleasant smile that truly captured attention, softening even the iciest of first impressions. Yet all the warmth he carried could not spare him from the rough and sometimes treacherous road of starting over in a foreign land.

His first stumbling block, unsurprisingly, was his name. After a few valiant but hopeless attempts to pronounce it, the locals simply threw up their hands and settled on calling him "Toot." Tuất, with bigger worries pressing on him, like finding work, learning a new language, and somehow building a life from almost nothing, accepted the name without complaint. It was a small thing to surrender, given how much else he had already left behind.

Together with his wife, he owned and managed three thriving nail salons nestled in the heart of Winnipeg, a Canadian city so cold it was often likened to the distant, frozen stretches of Siberia.

The opening of their third shop stood out in Tuất's memory. The date hadn't been chosen on a whim; it followed careful consultation with a fortune teller based two thousand miles away, in the Vietnamese enclave near Los Angeles. She had sent Tuất an urgent fax, proclaiming that the stars would align perfectly on that day, marking it as auspicious for new beginnings. The new salon was named 'Bamboo Shoot 3,' following their earlier two, 'Bamboo Shoot 1' and 'Bamboo Shoot 2.' The name was a quiet tribute to his wife, or more precisely, to the way he adored her hands. To Tuất, they embodied the essence of feminine grace: slender, elegant, and gently curved, like the tender sprout of a young bamboo shoot, as the old Vietnamese saying goes.

The new shop was more than just another business milestone. It stood quietly as a testament to how far Tuất had come, in both distance and spirit. Hard to believe that less than twenty years earlier, he had been among the first wave of Vietnamese refugees to set foot on Canadian soil. At just seventeen, he stepped off a plane at Winnipeg International Airport with little more than a bewildered heart and a pair of Japanese sandals that went 'squish-squish' with every nervous step across the polished floor.

When Ann Blankart, a reporter from the 'Winnipeg Tribune', caught wind that Tuất was about to open his third salon, she wasted no time tracking him down. She wanted to feature him in a feel-good story about an immigrant building a new life in a new land. She even had a title ready: 'From Rags to Riches.'

Tuất chuckled at the idea. He understood the general gist, something about starting poor and ending up rich, but the phrase 'rags to riches' puzzled him. Rags? Riches? It sounded like one of those colorful sayings Canadians liked to toss around, and he wasn't quite sure he fit the picture they had in mind.

Rags? Yes, that part rang true enough. He could never forget those early days, starting life as a teenage apprentice mechanic in a suburb of Saigon, nearly homeless and covered in grease most days. Some things didn't scrub off so easily. He could still feel the old sting - the awkward glances, the forced smiles, the way people's eyes flickered away when they noticed the stubborn oil stains that once seemed to belong to his very skin.

But riches? That was hard to believe. Every day still came with its own set of worries: keeping the business afloat, feeding a growing family, saving for the children's education, patching up one dream while chasing the next.

Tuất didn't spend too much time second-guessing the meaning behind the phrase, or the reporter's intentions. He was more than happy to accept the interview, seeing it as a golden opportunity to promote his salons. During the interview, Ann asked numerous probing and at times deeply personal questions. Tuất, however, felt he had answered them all thoroughly, embracing the straightforwardness typical of a Southern Vietnamese, telling it like it is, divulging everything, and holding nothing back. Most of her questions centered on his professional journey in Canada.

After nearly an hour of lively conversation, Ann smiled and told Tuất there was just one final question.

"Please share with our readers an important event or moment from your past that you believe marked a turning point in your life."

Immediately, a thought flashed through Tuất's mind: 'The flashlight.'

Fortunately, he caught himself before saying it aloud. Had he blurted it out, Ann might have smiled politely and asked whether he was experiencing a short circuit. It would have been understandable - without context, the answer would have sounded baffling. Explaining it properly would have taken far more time than the moment allowed. Setting aside the memory of the flashlight, Tuất instead used the opportunity to express his gratitude to the kind-hearted Canadians who had once warmly embraced him and his fellow compatriots during their early days in a foreign land.

Many hectic days later, the journalist's final question still echoed in Tuất's mind. It hadn't been a surprising or difficult question - the sort reporters often use to unearth scandals or uncover hidden truths. On the contrary, it was a routine, harmless inquiry meant only to satisfy the gentle curiosity of her readers. Tuất believed he had responded well, even managing to sprinkle in a bit of humor to end the conversation on a light-hearted note. He hoped the interview had left a pleasant impression on the warm-spirited journalist. More importantly, he hoped it had resonated with the loyal readers of the popular column '*A Stroll Around the City with Ann*', which appeared daily on page three of the newspaper.

There was something about the journalist's last question that lingered longer than expected. Though simple on the surface, it swept Tuất off his feet and carried him halfway across the world, back to a time and place steeped in the scent of river silt and straw smoke. In an instant he was no longer in snowy Winnipeg but standing barefoot on sun baked earth in the Mekong Delta, reliving the moment that changed everything. That single event, so long ago yet still vivid, hadn't just nudged him onto a new path - it had hurled him into a life story more improbable than anything he had ever read in a novel. And now, like a film reel unspooled in his mind, it all began again.

This morning offered a rare and precious opportunity for daydreaming. The snowstorm from the night before had kept the usual flow of customers away, leaving the world outside swaddled in soft, dazzling white. The stillness of it all lulled Tuất into a reverie stirring memories of a distant past and unforgettable moments he held closest to his heart. He retreated to the small office tucked behind the nail salon and slumped into a chair, casually propping his feet atop piles of receipts scattered across the desk. His gaze drifted absently toward the glass window, seeking a few stolen moments of escape.

Before long, following a quiet ritual of his, he reached over and pressed play on the cassette player tucked into the corner. Whenever the shop fell silent, he would let Vietnamese music fill the room, allowing the familiar melodies to carry him away.

The captivating voice of Diva Hương Lan soon enveloped the space, drawing Tuất deeper into his memories. The mellifluous tunes transported him into a dreamscape where his soul found solace and distant recollections blossomed. Oh, Hương Lan's voice! It was like a cool breeze swaying a hammock on a summer afternoon beneath the lush canopy of mangosteen trees in the gardens of Lái Thiêu. Her songs conjured visions of a freshwater boat, eagerly awaited by gentle souls along the banks of the Salted Water Canal. They summoned images of red, glossy plums, reminiscent of the plump cheeks of a vendor girl standing behind a fruit stall at the bustling Trung Lương bus stop, at the gateway to the western rice fields. They brought forth visions of white storks soaring gracefully into the endless sky as the bus rumbled away from Bình Điền Bridge, bound for the heart of the Mekong Delta.

And then, as if drawn from some tender corner of memory, there came the image of a small glass of juice made from the sap of the Trôm tree (Sterculia foetida), delicately sweetened with alum sugar. A humble, revitalizing elixir, lovingly offered by a sweetheart, capable of lifting the spirit of a weary soldier stationed at a distant military camp.

As Tuất drifted along the river of dreams, carried by the voice of Hương Lan, the sky within him seemed to unfurl. From its expanse poured a cascade of golden sunshine, warm and familiar, wrapping itself around his soul like an old embrace from home.

Outside the window, the world lay beneath a sea of dazzling white. Snow blanketed the streets, the fences, and clung to the trunks of trees, each branch bowed under winter's silent weight. Yet strangely, the frost did not numb Tuất's longing for home. On the contrary, it stirred something deep within, warming the well of childhood memories he kept close to his heart.

The sight of snow-laden apple branches called to mind the delicate white netting that cradled the tender stems of water mimosa, floating gently in the ponds and lakes of Long Kiến commune, in Chợ Mới District, An Giang Province, the very heartland of his youth. From that memory surged the vivid taste of water mimosa steeped in the savory richness of fish sauce, the way his grandmother used to prepare it in her braised dishes. A single flavor, a single scene, enough to bring an entire world rushing back.

Tuất's mother hailed from a village just across from his father's, both nestled on Ông Chưởng Islet, embraced by the gentle currents of the Hậu River. The area was famed for its abundance of fish and shrimp, so plentiful that even the birds seemed to spread the word, inspiring a playful local folk song: 'Three times the crow tells the kite / There are plenty of fish and shrimp left on Ông Chưởng Islet.'

Tuất couldn't say for certain just how abundant the fish truly were, but a story his grandmother once told had left a lasting impression. During the flood season, fish from Cambodia's Tonlé Sap Lake would surge downstream with the rising waters, spilling into the fields and replenishing the land. Villagers would wade into the flooded paddies with baskets, gathering fish to take home for drying or fermenting into salted fish, known as 'pissalat'. Sometimes, while carrying two baskets suspended from the ends of a shoulder yoke, the weight would grow too heavy. To ease their burden, they would stop along the way, pull out the biggest fish from each basket, and toss them aside without a second thought.

Thinking of salted fish brought back to Tuất the sweet aroma of snakehead tails used to soften the sharp saltiness of a braised fish sauce - his grandmother's specialty whenever relatives came to visit. She would always set aside two tender prawns from the dish and place them gently in Tuất's rice bowl, making sure he didn't lose his favorite morsels to the faster hands of the other children. After the meal, with the sun still high and the river calling, he would join cousins from both his uncle's and auntie's sides, racing down to the riverbank. There, they would clutch water-coconut sheaths or banana trunks for makeshift floats and plunge into the cool, sun-dappled water, their laughter rippling through the afternoon air.

In search of more fun, they would pile into a flimsy little boat and gently row along the narrow, winding canals, eyes peeled for water apples dangling from low branches. They knew just what to look for - those still half-ripe, tinged with green but already releasing a subtle, sweet fragrance. Once gathered, the fruits were carefully nestled in a rice jar overnight, left to ripen just enough to enjoy the next day. Though merely a childhood treat, the delight they found in those water apples rivaled the way adults savored a priceless mangosteen.

It was in that same land, where Tuất's sacred umbilical cord had been buried beneath the ancestral soil, that another memory took root, one destined to linger far longer and reach far deeper than the fleeting taste of any fruit. It was there that the story of 'The Flashlight' began, a moment that, in time, would come to define the turning point of Tuất's life. He was just sixteen, and it all began on the wedding day of his eldest brother.

It was a splendid morning. The ancient bamboos swayed joyfully in the breeze, their bright green leaves glistening under the golden sunlight. Though the countryside wore its usual face, something in the air felt different. The groom, Tuất's eldest brother, wore a bashful half-smile as he shyly walked alongside his bride, offering respectful bows to the gathered elders. Relatives, dressed in crisp, unfamiliar garments, carried themselves with quiet grace as they accompanied the bride on her ceremonial journey to her new home.

Tuất and the village children dashed through the grassy fields lining the path, eager to catch a glimpse of the bride in her vibrant 'áo dài, the traditional long dress that shimmered with each step. A tiny frog, perched on the edge of the bank, leapt into the ditch as the wedding procession approached. In the distance, a flock of storks, startled from their quiet foraging, took flight in graceful arcs across the sky. At the edge of a nest, a field crab retreated into hiding, much like the second aunt's youngest son, who blushed and hesitated at the bride's house as his mother nudged him forward to greet his new sister-in-law.

The grand wedding celebration unfolded in the front of the traditional three-section house inherited from Tuất's grandfather. Food and liquor flowed freely, and guests, young and old, rejoiced in the festivities that lasted well into the evening.

Before the sun had fully dipped below the horizon, Tuất's father stooped to place a lantern with an incandescent mantle at the center of the table. He stepped back and gave the oil tank a few pumps. Relatives and neighbors, both children and adults, gathered around to "watch the lights." They were not disappointed. A jubilant white flame flared to life, pushing back the dusk and banishing the darkness that usually cloaked the village. Apart from a few faint oil lamps flickering behind closed, weathered bamboo fences, the night seemed to yield entirely to the lantern's glow.

Tuất, in particular, was eagerly awaiting a surprise from Uncle Eight, the youngest brother of Tuất's father, who had long built a life for himself in Saigon and rarely returned home except for major occasions, like that day's wedding.

Whenever Uncle Eight visited, he came bearing gifts from the city, generously sharing them with relatives in the countryside. Everyone received something, whether large or small. In earlier years, when Tuất's grandparents were still alive, they were often given blankets, bottles of liniment, and a variety of medicines, each remedy tailored to soothe the ailments of old age.

Tuất's father was hoping for a bottle of French wine and a few packs of COTAB cigarettes - perhaps even a pouch or two of loose tobacco leaves and some rolling papers, so he could indulge, from time to time, in his stubborn habit of hand-rolling a smoke. Whispered thanks could also be heard from Tuất's mother, grateful to Uncle Eight's wife for sending new bolts of 'Mỹ A' fabric and a bit of 'soie' (silk) for tailoring clothes, along with a few jars of imported cosmetics - even though, truth be told, she hardly ever used them.

Such were the gifts nestled inside the rattan chest Uncle Eight had brought back from Saigon. He unpacked them right away upon returning to the ancestral house where he had spent his boyhood. Tuất, too, received a share, but to him, the notebooks, pens, and dictionaries felt routine - just part of the usual assortment of gifts for students. He knew to wait patiently until later in the night, when Uncle Eight would quietly call him aside and slip something far more exciting into his hands, something like a brand-new toy, fresh from the big city.

Tuất's excitement for this 'special' toy simmered beneath the surface, just as everyone else brimmed with anticipation for Uncle Eight's nighttime arrival and the unveiling of their own little surprises. As evening deepened, Uncle Eight finally arrived, stepping into the bright pool of lantern light with a phonograph in hand. Carefully, he placed it on the table, then lifted a jet-black vinyl record to eye level, inspecting its surface under the light. With a gentle puff to clear away any dust, he positioned it neatly at the center of the gramophone.

The room fell silent as the needle touched the record, and old-fashioned tunes began to fill the air. The previously tranquil space suddenly erupted with joyous smiles, echoing laughter and cheers, marking the pinnacle of celebration on this wedding day. Well, perhaps except for the bride and groom, who had their own peak of happiness elsewhere in the festivities!

Tuất's father poured tea to invite the in-laws and the elders. Uncle Two pulled his chair closer to the table, closed his eyes, and savored the song and its lyrics. He cleared his throat and asked,

"In which play is this song?"

Uncle Eight knew that his brother was a connoisseur of opera and must have been familiar with this play. He hesitated before answering,

"It's '*The Wife Who Was Never Married*' by composer Kiên Giang."

Uncle Two cleared his throat again and questioned,

"Today is the boy's wedding day, so why the song about a wife who never married?"

The father-in-law, sitting next to Tuất's father, chuckled,

"Well, as long as the word 'wedding' is in it, it's enjoyable to hear Brother Two."

A neighbor, Uncle Three, laughed and joked,

"Whether married or not, as long as there is Diva Út Bạch Lan, I'm happy."

Uncle Six, an acquaintance from the upper village, slurred his words from the effects of alcohol,

"And if there are a few verses from Diva Thanh Nga, I'd be more than delighted."

On a nearby plank, the women sat on sedge mats, gathered around a bronze betel nut bowl, which had been polished a few days ago and still shimmered in gold from the nearby oil lamp. Tuất's aunt called out,

"People on this side are waiting for Divo Hữu Phước, gentlemen."

This was how the evening unfolded. With tea still warm in their hands and rice wine not yet emptied from their cups, the pleasant exchange of words and glasses clinking in toasts became sporadic and eventually made way for melodious songs that echoed through the night, harmoniously blending with the fruit orchards and rice fields of this farmland nestled along the Mekong River.

The familiar song's melodies wafted through the air, stirring a sense of longing within.

'... *Đói lòng ăn nửa trái sim,*
Uống lưng bát nước đi tìm người thương.'

(... In my hunger I eat half a rose myrtle fruit,
Drink a bowl of water, before embarking on a journey to find the loved one...)

Thanh Nga's mellifluous voice carried the simple yet affectionate essence of a neighboring girl, smoothly guiding the listener through an enchanting landscape. It all began at the purple myrtle hill on the plateau of the Central Highlands, traversing towering mountains and deep forests, ultimately leading to the vibrant Mekong delta in the South, permeated with the longing of the early pioneers. People eagerly followed the wooden notes of the 'song lang,' setting the rhythm of the music that sometimes tugged at the hearts of adventurers, attempting to soothe the enduring homesickness rooted in their souls after generations of exploring the bountiful South.

Tuất and the children gathered around the dining table behind the adults, their attention shifting from the previous mantle light to a mesmerizing phonograph. Tuất was enthralled by the spinning record, closely observing the rhythmic movements of the needle and contemplating the origins of the sounds emanating from 'the singing machine.' Still curious and unsatisfied, Tuất felt a hand gently pulling his shoulder. Uncle Eight guided him to the back of the house.

He opened a paper bag, revealing a shiny aluminum flashlight, which he then presented to Tuất. Tuất gazed at this unexpected gift, a smile playing on his lips, and he offered a grateful bow. Without a word,

Tuất pointed the flashlight toward the darkest corner of the garden, beneath two thick mango trees that seemed to engulf all light from the moon and stars. Eagerly, he searched for a switch, a button, anything to ignite the flashlight, yearning to defy nature and illuminate a mango tree at night with just a small object held in his palm.

From the mango tree to the towering bamboo, and from the rig for melons to the chicken coop, a mysterious column of light gracefully danced across the garden, illuminating every nook and cranny in the playful hide-and-seek game with nature. Uncle Eight stood nearby, radiating joy and sharing in the youthful eagerness to explore the world, much like a playful puppy exploring its surroundings, sniffing at everything and barking at its newfound delights. All of this occurred under the watchful eyes of a devoted follower, the mother dog, lazily reclining in a corner, keeping a vigilant eye.

For the entire week, Tuất and his flashlight were inseparable, akin to a person and their shadow. During the first two nights, he wandered around, holding a flashlight in his hand, exploring the fields and gardens guided by its light, showcasing its ability to dispel the menacing shadows. On one occasion, it led Tuất to a face-to-face encounter with what he had always feared, an ogre rumored to live deep inside the bamboo thicket behind his house, a story his grandmother had ingrained in him through a repeated childhood fairytale. However, to his relief, it turned out to be nothing more than a massive frog with wide eyes, far from the terrifying ogre of Thạch Sanh's legend.

As the inquisitive light accidentally illuminated a mound of human excrement beneath the brocade tree by the river, a spot where, in his daily routine, Tuất would seek relief for his digestive system, it triggered a moment of apprehension. In rural areas, it's not uncommon for children to harbor fears of ghosts and malevolent entities. Interestingly, these fears seem to evolve with the changing seasons. Not long ago, the fear was centered around blood-sucking vampires, but recently, the dread had shifted to voracious ogres who supposedly consumed one's entrails if they found his excrement at night.

Despite growing older, especially after entering high school, Tuất had become more composed regarding the unseen world that often haunted his thoughts at bedtime. Nonetheless, armed with a flashlight, he still sought to validate these unfounded fears. Tuất desired reassurance that the remnants of the day remained undisturbed, providing him with a sense of peace, knowing he would survive yet another night!

In the upcoming days, Tuất's fascination with seeking out ghosts waned, shifting instead to a newfound love for standing at the field's edge and gazing at the vast emptiness. Holding the marvelous device aloft, he directed its light into the night sky, captivated by the wondrous column of light. Against the backdrop of darkness, Tuất stood contorted, arched his back, and tilted his face skyward, tracing the path of the light until it vanished into the void. He stood in rapt stillness, pondering the origins and essence of light.

Recollections of the rainbow's beauty, often gracing the sky after rainfall, surfaced in Tuất's thoughts, along with a memory from fifth grade. It was a visit to Teacher Trí's home, where he had explained the enigmatic concepts. He spoke of white light from the sun and the mesmerizing phenomenon of refraction, wherein colored light rays combined to form white light, diverging at varying angles. Though the complex terminologies Teacher Trí used remained beyond Tuất's immediate comprehension, the scientific explanation had left an indelible mark in his memory.

Everyone seemed to understand the irresistible pull of light - its power to lift spirits, illuminate paths, and draw people toward it - just like the old saying, '*Saigon's street lamps light up the city in greens and reds*,' evoking the spellbinding charm of a bustling metropolis.

That idea had always resonated with Tuất. The elegant flashlight he once held wasn't just an object. It sparked a thrill within him, a quiet yet persistent flame of wonder and aspiration. From that moment on, the light became more than a glow in the dark; it was a symbol of the distant horizons he longed to reach.

2. The Turning Point

The flashlight Tuất had received from Uncle Eight from Saigon quickly became his most treasured possession. Its beam did more than illuminate the narrow paths and shadowy corners of the fields - it ignited within him a quiet yearning to go beyond, to pursue the unknown, the distant, the dazzling. In a rural hamlet where electricity remained a distant dream, the flashlight shimmered like a fragment of another world. Each night, it accompanied him on solitary walks beneath the stars, as he watched the drifting clouds and dreamed of places far beyond the paddies. But just as this small light had brightened his world, it would soon be abruptly extinguished, an unexpected loss that would mark a quiet yet pivotal turning point in his life.

That very afternoon, just after finishing his meal and before even setting down his chopsticks, Tuất sprang to his feet and hurried off to collect straw for burning, hoping to smoke out the mosquitoes from the buffalo stables before nightfall.

His recent burst of diligence hadn't gone unnoticed. For several days now, Tuất had been taking on chores without being told, and it stirred something tender in his father's heart.

"As Tuất gets older, he seems to be turning a new leaf," the old man remarked with quiet satisfaction.

Bánh, Tuất's third brother, couldn't suppress a smirk.

"Thanks to Uncle Eight's flashlight, Dad."

Their father raised an eyebrow. "Oh? What's that supposed to mean?"

Leaning in, Bánh spoke with a tone of playful certainty.

"These past few nights, he's been heading out into the fields with that flashlight, not really to check on the buffaloes like he says, but to stargaze."

The old man let out a chuckle. "So he wasn't worried about the rain or the mosquitoes?"

"Well, maybe a little," Bánh replied. "But mostly, he's been chasing the sky."

Suddenly, Bánh perked up with an idea.

"After that big rain this afternoon, the garden must be crawling with toads. Maybe tonight I'll borrow Tuất's flashlight to hunt a few - we could make green bean porridge for a late-night snack."

Their mother put down her chopsticks with a disapproving clink.

"There's plenty of food in this house. Why bother with those poisonous things?"

The father chimed in with a chuckle,

"If you've got a bottle of good rice wine to go with it, I won't stop you."

But the mother wouldn't let it slide.

"Did you forget about last year? Some folks in the neighboring village ended up in the hospital after eating toad meat. Lucky to be alive, I heard, it nearly killed them."

Bánh quickly scooped up the last grains of rice in his bowl and replied,

"They just didn't know how to prepare it, Mom. My friend Ngạn, a fellow buffalo herder, knows exactly how to do it. He chops off the head, skins it, removes the innards - what's left is fresh, white meat, really tasty. I've eaten it with him and his buddies several times. It's perfectly fine."

Bánh, anxious about lingering at the dinner table, worried his mother might find another excuse to keep him home. He quickly shoveled the last mouthful of rice into his mouth, set down his bowl, and stood up with a casual air that poorly masked his haste. Without waiting for any further objections, he turned and made for the front door.

He went straight to Ngạn's house, calling out from the front yard in a half-whisper, half-shout, careful not to wake the elders. Ngạn, the lanky buffalo herder with a sly grin and a reputation for bold ideas, came out quickly, already guessing what Bánh was up to. His younger brother, never one to be left behind, joined them as well. The three boys, brimming with mischief, headed down the dirt path to look for Tuất.

As they neared the village edge, they ran into Dần, a cheerful and talkative fellow who was always eager for company. "Where are you all off to?" he asked, bouncing with curiosity. When Bánh mentioned the toad hunt, Dần's face lit up, and without hesitation, he tagged along.

Just as they passed the buffalo stable, a soft glow flickered above the bamboo tops, a sure sign of a flashlight beam dancing through the thickets. That was Tuất. After a bit of convincing, he agreed to lend them his prized flashlight. With its steady, reliable beam lighting their way, the group set off confidently into the fields. Compared to the old days, when they had to rely on kerosene lamps with trembling flames easily snuffed out by the breeze, this was a luxury. The hunt was swift and successful. With sacks full of toads, they regrouped at an old shack behind Tuất's house, where they cooked up a pot of green bean porridge and kicked off their impromptu drinking party, passing around a bottle of rice wine someone had smuggled from home.

But the fears Tuất's mother had voiced earlier that evening, dismissed at the time as overcautious, soon turned chillingly prophetic. Fortunately, she had firmly insisted that Tuất stay home, keeping him from joining the fatal feast.

By morning, word spread like wildfire: several of the boys had fallen seriously ill. Some only suffered violent stomach cramps and fever, but others were not so lucky. Tragically, Dần died before dawn. The news cast a heavy shadow over the village.

Grief soon gave way to blame. Dần's heartbroken parents, overwhelmed by sorrow, quickly turned their anguish toward Tuất. Though he hadn't been present at the ill-fated gathering, rumors began to swirl. Some claimed they had seen him shining his flashlight toward the abandoned temple by the Ông Chưởng canal, a place steeped in old fears and avoided by many for its reputation as a haunted, sacred site. Whispers spread that he may have disturbed the spirits said to dwell there, angering them and inviting their vengeance upon poor Dần. As the village murmured and speculated, suspicion took root. Dần's grieving parents accused Tuất of bearing some hidden responsibility, insisting that the beam of light he cast had somehow guided their son into the shadows of misfortune.

Tuất's parents, moved by the sorrow that had befallen Dần's family and wary of judgment from neighbors, made a heartbreaking choice: they cast Tuất's beloved flashlight into the depths of a nearby river. The very river that had once brimmed with childhood memories now carried away a piece of his soul. That flashlight had been his faithful companion, gripped tightly each night by a boy driven by wonder and a longing to explore the world. Its loss carved a deep void in his young heart.

His parents understood this and felt his pain as if it were their own. They, too, were caught in the binds of circumstance, unsure how to ease the growing tension with the community without breaking their son's heart. A quiet sorrow settled over the household, most keenly felt at the dining table, where Tuất's cries echoed with a familiarity that recalled the last time he had lost a beloved toy - only now, the grief ran deeper, more enduring.

After each meal, he would drift to the riverbank, standing alone on a high mound, eyes fixed on the horizon, releasing his thoughts into the water's current. He imagined the flashlight's voyage: its beam cutting through dark waters, journeying from riverbeds to the ocean floor, perhaps even finding its way to distant planets. In his dreams, Tuất chased that wandering light across the globe, much like Phileas Fogg in 'Around the World in 80 Days', a translated tale that had once captured his imagination. The story lingered in his mind, each chapter a window into strange lands, unfamiliar peoples, and fantastical adventures - the worlds he longed to see, if only in dreams.

At school, Tuất struggled to shake off an overwhelming sense of loneliness, made worse by the quiet distance kept by his classmates, especially Dần's two younger brothers. Once, his friends from the village had eagerly sought his company, but now they hovered at arm's length. They didn't blame him outright, yet the warmth in their eyes had faded, replaced by something more guarded. The joyful gatherings beneath the flamboyant tree on the school lawn, where they once affectionately called one another 'brother' and 'sister', now seemed like distant echoes of a time long gone. A heavy sorrow settled in Tuất's heart. He regretted ever lending the flashlight to his brother, a gesture that had, in some cruel twist of fate, driven a wedge between him and the friends he once held dear.

The sense of isolation and the weight of guilt clung to Tuất, shadowing his mealtimes and disturbing his sleep. Even his parents' daily words of encouragement, once meant to inspire, now rang hollow. *"You must persevere in your studies for a better future,"* they would say. Or, *"Try to pass the national exams so you can become somebody in society."* But young Tuất had never aspired to prestige or power. Those ideals seemed more distant, almost irrelevant to the dim world he now inhabited.

With the loss of his flashlight, he had also lost the light of intellectual curiosity. Each day, the boredom deepened, and whatever spark remained in him slowly dimmed. He no longer felt drawn to the well-trodden path laid out before him. A life marked by standardized success, climbing from high school to college, from diploma to degree, as though one's fate had been decided in advance. In this world, people clung to the idea of education as salvation, building for themselves an illusory paradise in the short span of a human life.

Within this system, a middle school diploma could elevate you above the lowest ranks, qualifying you as a junior officer rather than a mere foot soldier. A bachelor's degree brought honor, securing a position as a reserve officer and earning your parents' pride. A second degree might open the gates to a prestigious military academy, where you could ascend to the rank of a full officer, perhaps even dream of becoming a general one day. With a pharmacy degree, you could simply lend your name to a businessman running a drugstore and collect twenty thousand piasters a month without lifting a finger. And perhaps best of all, a medical degree could win you not only social respect, but also a beautiful wife and, as the saying goes, "a few well-raised children."

The idea had begun to take root in Tuất's mind: perhaps the only way forward was to leave. He dreamed of going to Saigon to live with Uncle Eight, though the thought was tangled with worry. What if his uncle disapproved of his decision to abandon home? Uncle Eight had once promised to support Tuất's education, but only on the condition that he finish high school in his home province first. Tuất, however, no longer felt he had the patience to wait for that day. The weight of waiting, of trudging through an uninspiring routine, had become too much. He longed to fill the growing void of meaninglessness with wonder, with anything that could spark life into his spirit.

29

3. The Early Days Of The Wanderer

Tuất's journey didn't begin with a plan, only with a quiet yearning, a longing for something beyond the muddy trails and rice paddies of his native hamlet. The decision had taken root in his heart long ago, silent and steady, like the hidden tangle of mangrove roots beneath murky waters. That yearning grew with every clever toy, every puzzling gadget brought home by his uncle from the big city. Each one whispered the same message: there's a world out there, mysterious and thrilling, waiting to be discovered.

There was no tearful goodbye, no dramatic farewell. Just a note quietly slipped beneath a pillow, and a morning that looked no different from the rest. Tuất rose with the dawn, slung his satchel over his shoulder, and set off as if for school. But this time, his bag held no textbooks, only two sets of new clothes and a small compass tucked deep into the folds.

And so, with little more than a restless heart and the vague hope that his uncle might take him in somewhere in Saigon, Tuất began his journey. He didn't know where he would sleep or what he would do. All he knew was that he had to go.

He paddled his sampan for nearly half an hour along the familiar canal, just as he had done every morning on his way to school. When he reached Uncle Two's land, he moored the boat to a weathered coconut tree and set off on foot. The water mimosa swamp he passed through, once a quiet comfort in his daily routine, now felt like it was offering a soft, unspoken farewell.

As Tuất walked, anxiety clung to every step, dimming his usual delight in the small wonders that once brought him joy. He passed the pond without noticing the tiny golden ladybug, its crystal-clear wings catching the light as it inched along a green water fern leaf. Nor did he feel the familiar thrill of spotting a green-and-yellow striped buffalo dragonfly, wobbling like a miniature helicopter atop a reed by the ditch.

Near the school gate, the fear of encountering friends, who might sense something was amiss, gripped him. His heart pounded, as if ready to burst from his chest. To steady himself, Tuất slowed down, taking a few mindful steps in an effort to calm his nerves. Then, with quiet resolve, he crossed the street, following the long shadows of the ancient tamarind trees lining the road. He turned toward Kiến An Market and quickened his pace toward the bus station.

Seated on the front bench of the Hiệp Hòa bus, waiting for departure to Saigon, Tuất hugged his school bag tightly to his chest. His gaze was locked on the horizon, where sunlight spilled through the side window in dazzling shafts, while a hundred thoughts spun restlessly in his mind. Outside, Mr. Tư, the bus driver, puffed on a cigarette between fits of coughing as he circled the vehicle, securing baskets and parcels from the vendor passengers stacked high atop the bus.

When Mr. Tư finally climbed aboard, Mrs. Bảy, seated just behind Tuất, leaned forward and asked:

"Hey, where's Lượm? Why isn't he helping you today?"

Mr. Tư settled into the driver's seat, lit another cigarette, took a long drag, and then replied wearily:

"He was drafted."

"When did that happen?"

"Just yesterday afternoon. When the bus reached the final checkpoint at Renault Bridge, the police claimed he was using counterfeit documents, so they took him away."

After his explanation, Mr. Tư erupted into another bout of coughing. Mrs. Bảy anxiously advised,

"You should find someone else to assist you. You're getting old. How could you manage to drive and handle the cargos all by yourself?"

Mr. Tư gazed outside, feeling fatigued,

"In this day and age, they've all been caught by the military. Where can I find another helper?"

The conversation about driver's helpers stirred up fond memories of a childhood pastime for Tuất. Back then, whenever the chance arose, he and a few fellow buffalo herders would row a sampan out to the Coconut Bridge, a modest crossing where the national highway met the village canal, just to "watch the passing cars." It was a simple pleasure: waiting by the roadside for the rare thrill of a vehicle rumbling past. After the initial excitement wore off, they would paddle back home, satisfied with the glimpse of a world beyond their fields.

In later years, as traffic grew more frequent, the sight of cars and buses lost its magic. Military convoys began appearing more often too, brimming with heavily armed soldiers. The tension they brought cooled the boys' curiosity and eventually put an end to those roadside outings.

And yet, one image from those days remained vivid in Tuất's memory: the bustling scene at the Coconut Bridge bus stop whenever a long-distance bus arrived. From afar came the low rumble of an engine, growing louder until the vehicle suddenly veered to the shoulder, kicking up a thick cloud of dust. What followed was a brief moment of chaos - shouts, rushed farewells, and promises yelled into the air before the dust had even begun to settle. Vendors hurried to gather their baskets and crates from the roadside. And there, like an actor on a stage, the driver's helper stood confidently atop the bus, steady as if on solid ground. With practiced ease, he shifted bundles, moving from side to side, calling out cheerfully to the crowd below: "Auntie Hai, pass the basket up here!" or "Grandma, go ahead and board. I'll bring it up in a sec!"

Before the bus pulled away, the driver's helper climbed down from the roof and took his position on the rear bumper, gripping the iron frame with practiced ease. Leaning out, he scanned the surroundings with sharp eyes, ensuring everything was in order. He even cast a long, deliberate glance down the dusty road and along the riverside path leading to the highway, checking for any stragglers. Only then did he give a final wave - his signal for the driver to depart. In young Tuất's eyes, the helper, agile and commanding as he managed the entire process from arrival to departure, resembled a field commander marshaling his troops.

Snapping back to the present, Tuất was surprised to find his bus already in motion, slowly rolling out of the city. The familiar fields flanking the road began to fall away, retreating into the distance, leaving behind a hollow ache in his chest. He clutched his school bag tightly, as if it were the last tangible link to a life he was being pulled from. The uncertain journey ahead weighed heavily on him, stirring a flood of questions: Would his uncle let him stay in Saigon? Should he endure the tedium of school, or set out to find work, though he hadn't the faintest idea what kind?

The bus pulled into the Trung Lương intersection, a major rest stop for buses traveling to and from the Western provinces. Passengers spilled out, heading toward roadside eateries or gathering around fruit stalls. Others stayed behind, unwrapping their packed meals. Tuất was among them. He knew his money was limited, just eighty piasters saved up from several years of New Year lucky money, so that morning he had made sure to eat an extra bowl of rice to stave off hunger.

Mr. Tư was seated outside a modest tea stall, sipping tea and leisurely smoking on a low stool. Tuất spotted him and hesitated, watching him for a moment, unsure of whether to approach. At last, summoning his courage, he stepped off the bus and walked over.

Before sitting down, Tuất asked,

"Do you need a driver's helper, sir?"

Mr. Tư looked up, surprised.

"Not really. Why do you ask?"

"I overheard you talking to that passenger back at the station," Tuất explained.

Realization dawned on Mr. Tư's face.

"Ah, you mean when I mentioned my helper being drafted? I didn't want to go into it earlier. Today's actually my last day driving. Tomorrow I'm returning the bus to the owner for good. But I suppose the company will find a new helper soon enough."

Tuất lowered his head in disappointment. Mr. Tư studied him for a moment, his gaze sweeping from head to toe as if casting a spotlight.

"So, you were hoping to apply for the helper position?" he asked.

Caught off guard, Tuất gave a nervous smile and turned away, unable to meet the old driver's probing eyes. His gaze drifted to the bus idling by the roadside, and a pang of regret tightened his chest - a missed chance at a dream he hadn't dared to voice aloud.

Mr. Tư took a slow drag from his cigarette and spoke again.

"Still in school, huh? I suppose after so many lean years, you're hoping to find work to help support the family?

Tuất felt a quiet wave of gratitude toward the driver, whether by kindness or instinct, Mr. Tư had offered him a graceful way out. Tuất gave a small nod in response, wordless but clear.

After the short break, the bus resumed its route. It had passed Bình Điền Bridge and was approaching the final checkpoint at Renault Bridge before entering the Saigon station. Tuất slumped over his school bag, a weight of uncertainty pressing on him, when Mr. Tư's voice rose again from the front.

"Hey, can you teach? I know a family that's looking for a tutor. Their kid's about nine or ten."

Like a drowning man grasping a lifebuoy, Tuất shot upright and leaned eagerly toward Mr. Tư.

"So the child's in fourth or fifth grade, right, Mr. Tư?"

"Most likely," the driver replied with a nod.

A smile broke across Tuất's face, brushing away the shadow of worry that had clung to him all morning. His eyes lit up with renewed hope as he said quickly, "Please, Mr. Tư, could you introduce me to them?"

Mr. Tư nodded again, this time with warmth, and recited the address Tuất could visit the next day. Tuất leaned back into his seat, stretched his legs, and let the wave of relief and excitement wash over him. Not only did he feel confident in his abilities, but he was genuinely eager for the opportunity. He had spent the past few years tutoring Aunt Sáu's two boys, helping them prepare for their high school entrance exams - the experience that now felt like a solid foundation.

At last, the bus reached its final stop at Saigon Station. Without being asked, Tuất climbed up onto the roof to help unload the passengers' luggage. In a matter of minutes, the once bustling bus stood empty, hollow from top to bottom. The crowd had dispersed in all directions, and only Mr. Tư remained, leaning against the door, quietly counting his earnings and wrapping up the day's work. All that was left now was to return the bus to its owner, one last time.

Before boarding the bus, Mr. Tư caught sight of Tuất standing motionless beneath a streetlight, looking lost and adrift. His eyes were fixed on a small piece of paper, likely an address he was struggling to locate. Years of scraping by on the road had taught Mr. Tư to recognize the signs of someone in a tight spot. There was something about the boy that had inspired his trust from the very beginning. Without pressing for details, he quietly extended a lifeline:

"If you need a place to stay tonight, you're welcome to stay at my place."

Tuất hesitated for a moment, then nodded, accepting the offer with heartfelt gratitude, as if reaching for the hand of a rescuer. He quickly followed Mr. Tư onto the bus, closing out the first day of his journey, one that had gone relatively smoothly, save for the occasional dark cloud and distant thunder rumbling within him.

Still, his body felt lighter, as though a burden had been lifted. He leaned back in his seat, letting himself sink into a quiet daze, barely noticing the way the bus wound through the maze of city alleys, carrying a young traveler toward an uncertain horizon.

After returning the bus to the company, Mr. Tư led Tuất on a good twenty-minute walk to his home. The house, with its rust-red tiled roof casting shadows over moss-colored walls, was where Mr. Tư always returned after each long journey. Though modest in size, its location on the western outskirts of Saigon, in a semi-rural area, meant it was surrounded by a lush garden and abundant greenery. Just past a gate fashioned from intertwined dry branches lay a smooth dirt path leading to the house. On one side stood a guava tree, and on the other, clusters of pale yellow star gooseberries clung to their slender branches, drooping under the weight of fruit.

Approaching the front door with Mr. Tu, one would notice a curtain swaying gently in the evening breeze. At first glance, it resembled a traditional bamboo blind, but it was actually made of paper, pages from 'Free World Magazine', a publication once circulated in South Vietnam during its alliance with the United States. The magazine, meant to showcase American life, modern society, and scientific achievements, featured striking visuals printed on glossy, high-quality paper with vibrant inks and meticulous craftsmanship, so captivating that even its discarded pages found new life here.

For local residents, owning such luxurious items was a rarity. After reading 'Free World Magazine', many found it too precious to discard and looked for creative ways to preserve it. One popular method was to repurpose its glossy pages into faux bamboo blinds. Each colorful sheet was carefully cut into three strips, then meticulously folded and tightly rolled into small cylindrical tubes, about the size of a pinky finger. Each tube formed a "bamboo segment," and by threading thin zinc wires through their hollow centers, people could link them into long chains.

Multiple chains of these paper "bamboo" tubes were then strung together to form a full curtain. With genuine bamboo blinds, it was common to paint a scenic landscape across the surface, often seen hanging at the entrances of shops. But with the paper version, the result depended entirely on the preexisting images and colors from the magazine itself. To the right set of eyes, this collage of fragmented ads, photos, and bold lettering could resemble an abstract or even cubist painting, unintentionally striking and deeply admired in its own way.

Mrs. Tư and her youngest daughter, Hoa, were tending to the stove, busily preparing the evening meal. Mr. Tư stepped into the kitchen to remind his wife to cook an extra portion for their guest, then changed into shorts and led Tuất out back for a quick wash beside the old rainwater jar.

It wasn't until they all sat down to eat that Tuất finally had a chance to greet Mrs. Tư and meet Hoa properly. With hair gently streaked with gray and a round, gentle face lit by a warm smile, Mrs. Tư reminded him of his own mother.

After Mr. Tư finished recounting the story of how he'd come across Tuất earlier that day, his wife turned to their guest with a curious smile.

"So, you're from Long Xuyên? I'm from Lấp Vò - just a stone's throw away."

Seated beside her, Mr. Tư, clinging to a habit he knew wasn't ideal, added a pinch of sugar to his second shot of rice wine. He squinted as he took a sip, then let out a slow, fiery breath with the finesse of a seasoned drinker. Placing the cup back on the table, he gave his wife a sideways glance and quipped,

"Not 'that' close, darling. It used to take me nearly an hour to drive from one to the other. You and your habit of claiming kin with anyone the slightest bit refined!"

Mrs. Tư was not one to back down easily.

"You say it wasn't close? Back then, you used to hitch a ride on the bus from Long Xuyên all the time just to see me!"

Mr. Tư slumped onto the stool, his gaze drifting toward the past. A slow smile spread across his face as memories, fueled by the liquor, drifted in like a gently rocking boat. He leaned over to hug his wife, who blushed and pulled away, scolding, "You're too much. We have a guest in the house, remember?"

'Well,' he thought, 'why did you have to remind me of the happiest days of my life?'

Back then, he had been the same age Tuất was now. It was his first time living away from home, working as a driver's helper on the Mỹ Tho–Long Xuyên route. One day, when the bus stopped at the Lấp Vò market to pick up passengers, he was busy loading luggage onto the roof when he suddenly felt a gaze fixed on him.

Those eyes, so sweet, so bright, belonged to a girl selling sugarcane stalks by the roadside. Her glance was like the taste of the juice itself: tender, refreshing, and impossible to forget. His heart skipped a beat. That sweetness soaked into his soul and lingered with him all the way back to the Long Xuyên bus station. It wouldn't let him rest.

Without thinking twice, he rushed to the driver, who was just about to make the return trip, and asked for a free ride back to Lấp Vò, just to find the girl selling sugarcanes on the roadside.

Since then, after every trip to Long Xuyên, he would routinely retrace the journey of his heart. And from then on, one would often see a cheerful village girl standing by the roadside, selling sugarcane, while he, a bus helper, sat back, peeling sugarcane on the cement porch. Oh, the memories of first love. Mr. Tư dreamily savored the timeless taste of sugarcane, still lingering. In that bittersweet moment, intoxicated by both alcohol and love, he gleefully shared his happiness with the world. He glanced mischievously at Tuất for a moment and jokingly said:

"When you secure a stable job, I'll let you marry my daughter."

"There you go again," Hoa retorted in annoyance, setting down her chopsticks and leaving for the back porch. Mrs. Tư chuckled, addressing Tuất,

"You must be born in the Year of the Dog, as indicated by your name. Hoa is a year younger than you, then."

Tuất was embarrassed, not sure what Mrs. Tư meant. Luckily, at that moment, Mr. Tư staggered to his feet and said:

"Alright, I'm off to bed. You can take the cot outside to the garden for a cooler sleep."

Tuất lay on the canvas of the makeshift bed under the trellis filled with dangling long green melons, seemingly within reach. In the serene night, the golden moonlight seeped through the heart-shaped leaves swaying in the wind, casting a play of light and shadow, bringing the essence of the hometown sky into Tuất's heart. He softly recited a few verses from the poet Tản Đà's The Art of Enjoying Life:

'Trời sinh ra bác Tản Đà
Quê hương thời có, cửa nhà thời không
Nửa đời Nam, Bắc, Tây, Đông
Bạn bè sum họp, vợ chồng biệt ly
Túi thơ đeo khắp ba kỳ
Lạ chi rừng biển, thiếu gì gió trăng
Thú ăn chơi cũng gọi rằng
Mà xem chửa dễ ai bằng thế gian
Hà tươi cửa biển Tu Ran
Long Xuyên chén mắm, Nghệ An chén cà...'

(Heaven gave birth to Tản Đà, the poet.
His homeland remained, but his home was lost in time.
Half a lifetime spent in the South, North, West, and East.
Friends gathered, spouses separated.
His bag of poems accompanied him through three regions.

No stranger to the forests and seas, nor a lack of the wind and moon.
It may be just a humble joy, but how many people can claim to have
it?
Fresh barnacles from the sea gate of Touranne.
Long Xuyên with its braised fish sauce, Nghệ An with its salted
eggplants.)

Oh, Long Xuyên!

Far from his hometown, Tuất softly recited a poem he had once
learned from his senior classmates at Thoại Ngọc Hầu High School.
The words stirred something deep within him. If a poet, someone who
had only passed briefly through Tuất's homeland, could feel such
affection for Long Xuyên's humble 'braised fish sauce', how much
deeper must Tuất's own bond be with that land of meandering rivers
and crisscrossing canals?

Overwhelmed by homesickness, he silently prayed that his parents
had found the note he'd hastily tucked beneath his pillow: 'I'm going
to Saigon. Staying at Uncle Eight's.'

And then, with the tender vulnerability of a wanderer who had come
to accept the earth as his bed and the sky as his roof, Tuất slowly
drifted into sleep.

Early that morning, Mr. Tư brought Tuất next door to introduce him
to Mr. Hai Sang, with the hope that Tuất could tutor the man's
youngest son. Though the two families were neighbors, their houses
were divided by a tall wall lined with shards of broken glass along
the top, a clear boundary. Yet, thanks to their shared roots in Mỹ Tho
province, Mr. Tư had earned Mr. Hai Sang's trust and had been
allowed to move in and rent the house that once belonged to Mr. Hai
Sang's gardener.

They arrived at the grassy front yard of the villa, near two tall
wrought-iron gates, just as a fierce chorus of barking erupted from

inside. The front door was slightly ajar, and a servant soon emerged, recognizing Mr. Tư. Using both hands and feet, the servant skillfully held back the dogs while prying the heavy gate open, creating a narrow passage just wide enough for one person to squeeze through.

Tuất, wary and wide-eyed, hesitated as he took in the sight of the growling German Shepherds. But the tension broke suddenly when the dogs recognized Mr. Tư and, with tails wagging, bounded around joyfully to greet the familiar visitor.

With his nerves settling, Tuất looked up, and was struck by the sight of the grand, two-story white villa towering before him, pristine and stately. He followed Mr. Tư toward the backyard, walking between two rows of meticulously pruned bonsai trees planted in antique porcelain pots. Each tree boasted its own elegant silhouette, their twisted trunks and canopy shapes evoking parasols or flowing calligraphy. The garden was a living gallery of luxury: ancient pine, plum, persimmon, lime, kumquat, and most prized of all, a rare collection of four-season flowering apricot trees.

Mr. Tư and Tuất had walked a long way to the backyard before they spotted Mr. Hai Sang, who had just finished his breakfast and was now sitting under the shade of a jackfruit tree, reading the morning paper. Looking up and spotting Mr. Tư, Mr. Hai Sang greeted him cheerfully:

"Getting started now, are you? I'm getting too old for all this driving."

Mr. Tư nodded with a smile.

"Yes, I returned the bus to its owner yesterday. So I'm free now. Just give me a call whenever you need me."

Upon hearing this, Mr. Hai Sang quietly rejoiced. He had been concerned that Mr. Tư might have taken a better-paying job elsewhere. With the war escalating, young men were being conscripted from all walks of life. In the past six months alone, three of Mr. Hai Sang's drivers had been drafted. Recently, he had begun to worry that Mr. Tư might also reconsider working for him.

Without wasting a moment, Mr. Hai Sang called out for Mrs. Sáu, the housekeeper, and asked her to fetch two sets of Mercedes car keys for Mr. Tư. Relieved that his driver situation was now under control, he turned to Tuất and said with a teasing grin:

"And who's this - your bus helper? Want to send him over to my garage? Most of the mechanics there have already been drafted. Only Brother Seven's still around. I heard he just found two new helpers the other day, but one of them looked like a gentle wind might knock him over. Don't think the poor kid's cut out for it."

Tuất listened with interest, a spark of curiosity flickering to life. Ever since he was a boy, he had enjoyed tinkering with mechanical things, taking them apart and putting them back together again. But before the conversation veered too far, Mr. Tư stepped in and gently steered it in a different direction, introducing Tuất as a tutor for his youngest son, Trọng.

After asking a few questions about Tuất's academic background and experience, Mr. Hai Sang agreed to let him teach Trọng on a trial basis, three sessions a week, one hour each, focused on mathematics. Tuất gratefully accepted, his face lighting up with enthusiasm as he thanked Mr. Hai Sang for the opportunity.

Mr. Tư, meanwhile, was expected to stay at the Hai Sang residence throughout the day to be on hand whenever the family needed a driver. While Mr. Hai Sang usually preferred to drive himself, the driver's main duty was to shuttle the children to and from school. Occasionally, Mrs. Hai Sang also required transportation to her family's pepper export company, either to meet with clients or manage financial accounts.

Before leaving, Mr. Tư asked Tuất to let his wife know that he would be coming home for lunch later. He also suggested that Tuất temporarily stay at their house until he could find a more permanent place to live.

As Tuất stepped out of the Hai Sangs' gate, he caught the sound of laughter drifting from a nearby car repair shop. He assumed it was the same garage Mr. Hai Sang had just mentioned and, driven by curiosity, decided to take a closer look.

The garage, owned by Mr. Hai Sang and managed by a seasoned mechanic named Mr. Bảy, primarily serviced taxis but also handled the occasional private car and vehicles from various American civil agencies operating in the region. Many of these belonged to volunteer groups or church missions, often bound for remote areas with rocky, potholed roads. Drivers, wary of the wear and tear from such rough terrain, frequently brought their vehicles in for repairs or preventive maintenance.

From the outside, the repair shop resembled an abandoned house standing beneath the broad canopy of a tamarind tree, casting its shadow across a weathered tin roof. Beneath it lay a wide concrete floor, spacious enough to accommodate three or four vehicles at a time.

One familiar face at the shop was Mr. Sáu, a ship navigator who often dropped by around noon to sip tea and watch the mechanics at work. His real name was Sáu Hương, but owing to his profession, guiding foreign vessels from the sea gate at Vũng Tàu to Bạch Đằng Wharf in Saigon, he had taken on the nickname "Sáu Navigator." His job provided a comfortable living for his family. Occasionally, if a ship needed to make an unofficial stop to pick up contraband or restricted cargo, he could earn a handsome bonus. It was enough to afford a white Renault, which he used to take his wife and children on seaside getaways to Cape St. Jacques, Vũng Tàu.

The car, though relatively new, was notoriously temperamental. Sometimes the engine would overheat so badly that steam hissed from under the hood. Mr. Sáu would have to pull over, wait for the engine to cool, top off the water, and then cautiously resume the trip. The steering wheel had a mind of its own, veering left and right as if refusing to go straight. Because of this, he was a regular at Mr. Bảy's garage and, over time, grew close to the mechanics there.

Even after retirement, Mr. Sáu kept visiting the shop daily, though he'd long since sold the finicky Renault. By then, he was practically part of the family at this garage. On one occasion, he even gave Mr. Bảy, the chief mechanic, a good-natured nickname. Mr. Sáu had noticed that regardless of the issue a customer came in with, Mr. Bảy would somehow circle back to suggesting a steering bar replacement. One day, after a customer had left, Mr. Sáu looked at him, shook his head, and said with a grin:

"I've got my eye on you. Maybe I ought to start calling you Bảy 'de Song', since you keep bringing up that 'bar-de-song' thing all the time!" ('Bar-de-song' being the Vietnamese mechanics' rendition of the French 'barre de direction', meaning 'steering bar.')

The mechanics burst into laughter when Mr. Sáu cheekily revealed what they jokingly called the trade's "best-kept secret." From that day on, Mr. Bảy was saddled with his new nickname, a timeless French moniker that carried a touch of aristocratic flair. As Mr. Sáu once explained with a mischievous grin, "Don't be fooled, my friends. In France, the word 'de' in a name means noble blood!"

That morning, like clockwork, Mr. Sáu finished his breakfast and coffee at home before making his usual stroll to Mr. Bảy's garage. He settled into his spot at the makeshift table - a tree stump left over from when the old tamarind tree had been cut down two decades earlier to make space for the expanding workshop. The stump had been sawed flat to resemble a tabletop. A weathered teapot, cradled in a brown coconut shell that served as a makeshift warmer, sat beside a transistor radio softly playing 'vọng cổ' melodies (Southern Vietnam's classical laments) from morning till dusk.

Four plastic chairs surrounded the stump, transforming it into an impromptu tea table where drivers could relax while their vehicles were being repaired.

On this particular day, Mr. Sáu's usual companion, Teacher Chín, had yet to arrive. So when he saw Mr. Bảy 'de Song' approaching for his usual smoke break, Mr. Sáu welcomed him with a cheerful smile and poured him a cup of tea.

Tuất lingered nearby, wanting to approach them to ask for a job as a mechanic's helper. But something held him back. He hesitated to interrupt the two elders, unsure of how to begin the conversation. After a moment's pause, he turned and quietly made his way back to Mr. Tư's house.

As he walked, Tuất mentally tallied his expected expenses. The salary Mr. Hai Sang had offered would barely be enough to cover his daily meals. And then there were other costs - rent, clothing, and basic necessities - that had only crossed his mind that very morning. Where would he find the money for those?

He knew he needed a better job, not only to meet his everyday needs but for a reason that reached deeper. The motivation had been sparked the day before, when Mr. Tư had gently suggested, "Perhaps, after so many lean years, you're hoping to find work to help support the family?" The question had been speculative, not a reflection of Tuất's exact circumstances, yet it struck a chord. It awakened in him a sense of duty he had heard others speak of, a child's responsibility to his parents, but until now, he had only understood it in theory, never truly felt it.

Now, Tuất began to dream of the day he could return to his hometown bearing gifts, just as he had seen his Uncle Eight do every time he visited from Saigon.

Back at Mr. Tư's house, Tuất took a moment to count the money he had. After setting aside a few piasters for emergencies, he went out to the backyard, where he ran into Mrs. Tư just as she was returning from the market. Without hesitation, he handed her the remaining sum, considering it an advance for his first month's meals.

Tuất chose to hand the money to Mrs. Tư instead of her husband for a reason that had stayed with him since childhood. He remembered how his mother used to praise Uncle Eight's thoughtful gesture - how, during his visits, he never gave money directly to Tuất's father. Instead, he would quietly ask his wife to slip an envelope into Tuất's mother's pocket, without a word.

While waiting for Mr. Tư to return for lunch, Tuất wandered curiously around the front yard, admiring each plant and blade of grass. Beside two chili plants - heavy with clusters of tiny red and green peppers in an earthen pot bound with zinc wire - grew rows of daisies, marigolds, and 'fingernail' plants, their dainty pink and purple blossoms proudly lining the ground near the house. Looking up, he spotted bell-shaped red plums swaying in the breeze, as if ringing softly in the wind, teasingly inviting children to come pluck them.

Tuất's thoughts began drifting toward the past when, from the corner of his eye, he sensed someone at the gate.

Hoa had just returned. She opened the gate and wheeled her bicycle into the yard, freezing mid-step upon seeing Tuất in the garden. She had assumed, based on what her father said over dinner the night before, that he was only staying for the night. Tuất turned and greeted her with a warm, "Hoa," as though they'd known each other for years. She lowered her face and replied softly, "Brother Tuất," then continued forward, parked her bicycle on the dirt path, and walked straight toward the back of the house.

As her white 'áo dài' (the traditional Vietnamese long dress, with a form-fitting bodice and long flowing panels over loose trousers.) fluttered behind her, Tuất had the sudden impression that if he had passed her on the street, he might not have recognized her.

At yesterday's dinner, though he'd known she was there, Tuất hadn't spared her even a glance or smile. Partly because his mind was in turmoil, but mostly out of a deep-rooted sense of propriety. How could he dare steal a look at the daughter of the man who had kindly taken him in?

And yet, he hadn't been immune to the quiet grace she carried. He had noticed the way her long hair flowed over her shoulders, and especially that familiar gesture - how she always tucked a few loose strands behind her ear. This day was no different. After parking her bicycle, she stepped back a few paces, tilted her head thoughtfully and cast a final, discerning glance at the bike. Then, with effortless grace, she tucked her hair behind her ear once more before turning and disappearing into the house.

The afternoon unfolded slowly, marked by the quiet rhythm of household routines and the soft rustling of leaves in the breeze.

After lunch, Mr. Tư returned to Mr. Hai Sang's house to resume his duties as a driver. Before leaving, he told Tuất to meet him at Mr. Bảy's garage at four o'clock for an apprenticeship interview he had arranged on Tuất's behalf.

While waiting, Tuất moved from beneath the melon trellis to seek cooler shade under a dwarf coconut tree, its crown heavy with clusters of green coconuts. The slender, ringed trunk arched gracefully over a meandering stream that wound its way around the back field of Mr. Tư's property.

From where he stood, Tuất caught a glimpse of Mrs. Tư bustling in the kitchen, completely absorbed in preparing rice cakes. This day, he discovered that she not only handled all the household chores but also made tri-colored cakes to sell at the market, occasionally switching things up with glutinous rice cakes.

His eyes drifted to the backyard, where he spotted Hoa at the millstone, grinding rice. On instinct, he rushed to offer a hand. Hoa had just finished washing the dishes and was now grinding glutinous rice into flour for her mother's cakes. She had fastened the millstone's T-shaped handle to two ropes suspended from a jackfruit tree branch and was steadily rotating the top stone with focused care.

Tuất noticed the task seemed a bit too demanding for Hoa, so he stepped in.

"Let me take over the grinding for a while. You can stand by and just let the millstone 'eat and drink.'"

Hoa chuckled but didn't argue. She stepped aside, keeping a close eye on the revolving stone, ready to add more rice or water as needed. Tuất began turning the heavy millstone. After a few steady rotations, he asked,

"What's so funny, Hoa?"

Still smiling, she replied,

"It's the way you said, 'Let the millstone eat and drink.'"

Tuất grinned. "What else would you call it?"

"My mom says 'Let the millstone eat' whenever it's time to add more rice," Hoa said. "But I've never heard anyone say 'Let it drink' before."

After speaking, Hoa gave a gentle nod, delicately swept her hair aside, and cast a sideways glance toward the revolving millstone. Tuất quickly turned his gaze to the yard and asked, a bit hurriedly:

"Earlier, did I see you coming back from school out front?"

"Yes."

"Which school do you go to, Hoa? Is it far from here?"

"I go to Mạc Đỉnh Chi High School. It's about a 15-minute bike ride."

As if something had just come to mind, Hoa added softly,

"I'm not very good at school, especially in math, so I don't dare ask Uncle Hai Sang to let me tutor his child."

Tuất blurted out without thinking,

"I think you're doing great, Hoa. After school, you still help your mom with all the housework."

Hoa gently lowered her head, brushed a few strands of hair aside, and tucked them behind her ear. Tuất was taken aback by the contrasting images that surfaced on her face. That gentle gesture seemed to sweep away the look of diligence and quiet industriousness from a face that appeared mature beyond her years. And then, just as quickly, it gave way to an expression of innocence, tinged with a playful lightness, like that of a carefree girl.

Tuất absentmindedly diverted his eyes toward the jackfruit hanging on the nearby tree. Meanwhile, his hands continued to push and pull at the handle to keep the millstone revolving. Hoa, after grinding the flour, steamed the soaked mung beans to make the stuffing for the sticky rice cakes.

Tuất stepped into the house, slipped on a pair of sandals, and got ready to head over to Mr. Bảy's garage for the job interview. He felt a familiar wave of anxiety wash over him, the same nervous anticipation he'd experienced when he first met Mr. Hai Sang to discuss the tutoring position. But this time, it was different. This felt like the beginning of a new and far more unfamiliar journey, one whose destination he couldn't quite imagine.

Fortunately, the meeting went well, and Mr. Bảy agreed to take him on as an apprentice at the garage. In hindsight, it turned out to be a greater stroke of luck than Tuất had anticipated, as his tutoring job ended less than three weeks later. He was replaced by a third-year university student majoring in science - an only son of a widow, and thus temporarily exempt from military service.

After a few months of vocational training, Tuất had come to see Mr. Bảy's garage as a second home. Although he still lived at Mr. Tư's house, he only returned there for dinner and to sleep. During the day, the garage became his world, a place where he was warmly embraced by the older regulars as if he were their own nephew. His gentle demeanor, respectful manners, and eagerness to help out earned him their affection. Mr. Bảy often spoke highly of Tuất, praising his energy and his readiness to take on tough, physical tasks without complaint.

Five or six years earlier, when business began to boom, thanks in part to repair referrals from foreign civilians and companies operating in Vietnam, Mr. Bảy had purchased a black-and-white television as a gift for his mechanics. It gave them a chance to enjoy 'cải lương', the beloved Vietnamese modern folk opera, during their breaks. Mr. Sáu *'Navigator'* enjoyed it too, though when no traditional music was on, he would sometimes switch to the American military channel to catch football games broadcast to lift the spirits of U.S. troops stationed in the region.

Tuất had just finished helping Mr. Bảy install a new brake system on a van belonging to the Evangelical Church. With the work done, he settled down at the tea table to rest, watch some television, and chat with Mr. Sáu 'Navigator.' The two had been getting along increasingly well. Tuất's natural curiosity often led him to ask unexpected questions that caught Mr. Sáu off guard, but in a good way. He found it refreshing, even endearing, and welcomed the chance to share what he knew. At times, these conversations became an outlet for Mr. Sáu to open up, allowing him to share stories and memories he didn't know how to express to anyone else.

That afternoon, Mr. Sáu switched the television to Channel 11 to watch one of the American sports programs typically broadcast for U.S. soldiers. By coincidence, the famous America's Cup sailing race happened to be on. Tuất watched in silence, captivated by the swift, elegant boats slicing across the waves. After a while, he asked:

"Do those boats have engines, Mr. Sáu?"

"I told you, they're sailboats," Mr. Sáu replied, amused. "Why would they need engines?"

Tuất furrowed his brow, deep in thought, and didn't even catch Mr. Sáu's reply. Seeing this, Mr. Sáu chuckled and teased:

"You're too wrapped up in your trade. Everywhere you look, you're hoping to find an engine to fix, aren't you?"

Tuất laughed and shook his head.

"No, it's not that. I just see those boats gliding so smoothly, like cars on the road and don't get how sailboats can move forward and backward like that."

Mr. Sáu raised an eyebrow. "You've got quite the brain on you. If you go to school and keep at it, maybe one day you'll become an engineer, eh?"

Assuming Mr. Sáu was joking as usual, Tuất pressed on, trying to explain himself.

"But seriously, Mr. Sáu, if they only use sails, they'd have to go wherever the wind blows, right? So where do they find such strange winds that can push a boat forward, and then backward, just like that?"

Mr. Sáu lifted his teacup, took a thoughtful sip, and nodded approvingly.

"You've got a good head on your shoulders. But here's the thing. Sailing isn't about waiting for the wind to push the boat from behind. It's more like flying a kite. You see, there's no wind blowing straight up from the ground, but the kite still floats and soars, doesn't it?"

"You mean the wind blows sideways, but it still lifts the kite upward?"

"Exactly," Mr. Sáu replied, setting his cup down. "That's the secret. With sailboats, the helmsman adjusts the sail constantly, swinging it from side to side, to catch the wind at the right angle. Sometimes, to move forward, you have to go in a zigzag: a little to the right, then a little to the left, and bit by bit, the boat makes its way ahead."

Tuất's eyes widened, and a radiant smile spread across his face, delighting Mr. Sáu "Navigator." 'It wasn't for nothing that I studied maritime engineering in France for a few years,' Mr. Sáu mused proudly. Squinting at Tuất with admiration, he said:

"You've got a very inquisitive mind. Most people I know tend to rely on gut feeling or instinct. That's important, sure, but intuition should always be tested through proper reasoning, using scientific method."

As he spoke, Mr. Sáu paused mid-thought to greet Mr. Ba, a familiar face who had just walked into the garage. Mr. Ba was here to check on his taxi. Unlike most taxi drivers, who had to rent their vehicles, Mr. Ba had managed to buy a secondhand cab using savings from selling off a few plots of land in Bình Chánh. He made a living driving it himself.

A regular at Mr. Bảy's garage, he was affectionately known among the mechanics as Mr. Ba "Ngược", or Mr. Ba "Reverse." He was an older man, with deeply tanned skin and a rugged face, though his ever-present grin and easygoing, country-style speech softened his rough appearance. It was a shame his nickname could be misunderstood. "Ngược" might suggest he was stubborn or contrary, but in truth, it came from his curious obsession with horse race betting.

Each week, Mr. Ba would swing by the Phú Thọ Racetrack in his cab to place his bets. In the evenings, he often stopped by the garage for a cup of tea, his mood plainly written on his face, sometimes beaming with joy, other times heavy with disappointment, depending entirely on how the horses had run that day. The funny thing was, win or lose, his explanation never changed: "The horses came back in reverse!" If the outcome matched his hopes, he won big; if not, he was wiped out. Over time, the nickname stuck, and everyone simply called him Mr. Ba "Reverse."

A young apprentice noticed Mr. Ba walking in, his face etched with worry. As usual, he called out, "Got kicked by the horse again today, Mr. Ba?"

"Horses've been kicking me hard lately," Mr. Ba grumbled. "But these past two days, I've had to leave my car here for repairs - couldn't even make it to the track."

Without another word, Mr. Ba headed straight to the back of the garage where his cab was parked. He stood anxiously beside Mr. Bảy, not daring to rush him, though his impatience was palpable. Mr. Bảy, still wrestling with the final bolt, tilted his head and met Mr. Ba's eyes, as if trying to ease the pressure. "Try the ignition," he said calmly.

Mr. Ba didn't hesitate. He slipped behind the wheel and started the engine with a jittery hand, then took off, heading straight for the racetrack to make up for lost time.

Tuất loved working at Mr. Bảy's garage. It fed his curiosity and deep fascination with machines. From time to time, he picked up clever tricks and tales from Mr. Sáu *"Navigator."* As much as he enjoyed the grease and gears of the garage, there was something else that made each day worth it. Every evening, after washing up with rainwater stored in barrels along the sidewalk, Tuất would feel a flutter of anticipation stir inside him, like a child hurrying home to open a long-awaited gift. That 'gift' was often no more than a passing glimpse of Hoa in the soft light of dusk, gently tucking a few strands of hair behind her ear, her face aglow like the first light of dawn slipping through morning mist.

One day, while quietly watching Hoa as she studied at the dining table, Tuất found himself softly reciting a rustic folk verse from his hometown:

'Anh đi lục tỉnh giáp vòng,
Đến đây trời khiến đem lòng thương em.'

(I've wandered through all six provinces,
And fate has led me here to love you.)

Afterward, he sank onto the cot beneath the fragrant melon vine, watching the heart-shaped leaves sway gently in the golden moonlight. His heart wrestled with the ache of forbidden love. The Tưs had embraced him like family, offering kindness, shelter, and trust. 'How could he possibly pursue their daughter?' he asked himself.

And yet, just a week earlier, while accompanying Mr. Bảy to the flea market to buy a fan, Tuất had dared to pick out a brand-new Parker pen for Hoa. Upon returning, in a gesture of honesty and restraint, he handed the pen to Mrs. Tư and asked her to give it to Hoa as encouragement in her studies.

Each evening after his shift at the garage, Tuất would return to their house. Some days, he helped grind rice into flour for cakes; other days, he mashed mung beans for the fillings. And later at night, he would lie on the same old cot, gazing once more through the melon vine's leaves, hoping the moonlight might offer some clarity, or at least a moment's peace for his quietly swelling heart.

4. Riding The Waves

Just as Tuất was settling into a new rhythm at Uncle Bảy's garage - as he fondly called him - where each day unfolded with predictable warmth, quiet familiarity, and a sense of growing peace, the country was suddenly thrown into an upheaval of unprecedented magnitude. That seismic shift would soon shatter his fragile stability and sweep him away, as if in a waking dream, to a place he had never imagined.

Under the scorching midday sun in Saigon, Mr. Sáu 'Navigator' sat alone at the 'tree' table in front of Mr. Bảy's garage, eagerly awaiting Teacher Chín, an elementary school teacher expected to drop by at any moment. He had spent the entire morning waiting, idly gazing through the garage gate at the road repair workers just beyond.

The rumbling steamroller crawled forward, flattening the freshly laid asphalt beneath its smooth, heavy drum. A hazy vapor curled up from its path, rising into the noon air and trailing behind a pristine black surface. Occasionally, pockets of hot air trapped beneath the asphalt expanded and hissed through tiny crevices, forming small, round bulges, like cheap glass marbles from some underprivileged kids, half-sunk and glinting faintly under the sun.

Just as Teacher Chín's silhouette emerged in the alley, Mr. Sáu quickly reached for the teapot and poured a fresh cup of tea in anticipation. Without delay, Teacher Chín removed his pith helmet and began vigorously fanning himself, trying to dry the sweat trickling down his neck.

"It's sweltering today. On my way here, I saw a group of kids swimming in the river - I almost felt like stripping down and joining them," he exclaimed.

Mr. Sáu chuckled. "Here, have some tea to cool off."

As he glanced toward the road, Mr. Sáu added thoughtfully, "While waiting for you, I was watching the workers repairing the road and wondered - if the Americans have already pulled out, as they claim, then why are they still fixing roads? Is it some kind of farewell gift, or just a fake withdrawal?"

Since 1965, the U.S. had begun deploying troops to Đà Nẵng, aiming to shore up South Vietnam, seen as a critical bulwark of the free world against communist expansion from the North. But only five years later, under President Nixon, the U.S. initiated a so-called "honorable withdrawal," which plunged the South into increasingly perilous circumstances. By early 1975, the military situation had grown dire. Among pessimists, there was a creeping sense that the South's fate hung by a thread.

Teacher Chín set the white pith helmet on his thigh and slowly raised the teacup to his lips, taking a small sip to clear his throat.

"The road repairs this time are being carried out by our own government," he began. "The real question is why now, especially when American aid has been nearly cut off."

He paused, deep in thought, then continued in a lower voice, as if carefully weighing his words.

"Maybe it's part of an effort to secure a supply route between Saigon and the Mekong Delta provinces."

Mr. Sáu raised an eyebrow. "Are you suggesting they're preparing to shift the front toward the West?"

"I'm just speculating," Teacher Chín replied. "But I heard yesterday that Xuân Lộc might not hold. If that's true, then we've effectively lost everything from Huế to the Central Highlands. And once they break through Xuân Lộc, there's only about a hundred kilometers left to Saigon. If it comes to that, our only hope may lie with the forces in the western provinces."

Mr. Sáu added grimly, "But from what I've heard, over the past few weeks, many of the troops stationed in the West have already been redeployed to the Central front."

"Well, whatever forces we still have, we'll need to reinforce them somehow," Teacher Chín acknowledged.

As if suddenly struck by a thought, Mr. Sáu leaned forward and asked,

"Do you think the U.S. might intervene at the last moment and turn the tide?"

Teacher Chín took another sip of tea, then looked up at the sky where dark clouds were beginning to gather. He replied thoughtfully,

"It feels like a matter of fate. Whatever they choose to do will depend on their own national interests - and how could we possibly know what those are?"

Mr. Sáu shook his head, a shadow of discouragement crossing his face.

"Yeah, I feel it in my gut too. I've been following the news in 'Time' and 'Newsweek'. Back then, the Americans were protesting the war so fiercely - day after day, calling on their government to bring the troops home. With that kind of pressure, I doubt any U.S. president would dare get involved in Vietnam again."

The two old friends exchanged a weary glance. Teacher Chín let out a sigh.

"As I grow older, time seems to slip by faster and faster. The days of the French, the Japanese, then the Americans - each era different, yet all passing swiftly… like a horse trotting past the window."

"Are you getting too pessimistic?" Mr. Sáu replied, refilling his friend's teacup. "Where there's a will, there's a way, you know."

They both turned their attention to the neglected wooden chessboard beside them, its darkened pieces worn from years of play.

A few days later, on a quiet morning, the garage sat empty. The street outside was unusually still, with no cars passing by. Only Rê and Ri were out as usual, kicking a soccer ball around the grassy field in front of Mr. Hai Sang's villa.

Tuất had been surprised the first time he saw them playing so energetically right after a meal - something he had always been taught to avoid for fear of appendicitis. Rê and Ri, who were around his age, played without a care in the world. Clad in nothing but black shorts, their round, firm bellies gleamed in the sun as they ran barefoot through the grass.

Tuất later learned they were Montagnards who had once worked on Mr. Hai Sang's pepper plantation and export business in Lộc Ninh, before being brought to the city to tend the villa's garden. On slow days at the garage, when there were no vehicles to repair, Tuất and a few of the apprentice mechanics would sometimes join the Rê brothers for a spirited soccer match.

With nothing to do, Tuất stood idly in front of the garage, watching Rê and his brother dribble the soccer ball back and forth. Nearby, Mr. Bảy 'de Song' sat gloomily on a tree stump, deep in conversation with Mr. Ba "Ngược." Suddenly, Mr. Bảy waved Tuất over.

"I've got a mission for you," he said curtly.

Tuất furrowed his brow. "What kind of mission, Uncle?"

The story had begun the night before. Mr. Hai Sang, fed up with overdue rent, had someone confiscate Mr. Bảy's toolbox, his most prized possession, as payment. After all, Mr. Bảy was three months behind on rent for the garage.

Mr. Bảy looked at Tuất, then spoke with hesitation. "You know the Rê brothers… You might be able to help."

Tuất looked puzzled. Mr. Bảy leaned in and lowered his voice to a whisper.

"Slip into Mr. Hai Sang's house and check if our toolbox is there."

Realization flickered across Tuất's face. "And if it is… you want me to bring it back?"

"Yes. If you find it, take it and bring it back."

Tuất hesitated. "Isn't that stealing, Uncle?"

"It's ours," Mr. Bảy replied firmly. "You're not stealing - you're just taking back what belongs to us."

Since the American troops had started to withdraw more than two years ago, the auto repair shop had grown increasingly quiet. Fewer and fewer cars were brought in for service, and in recent months, business had become especially sparse. As a result, Mr. Bảy was no longer able to pay the garage rent as regularly as he once did.

Last night, Mr. Ba Ngược had brought his car in for repairs, only to find that several essential tools were missing. All morning, Mr. Bảy had wrestled with the problem, unsure of what to do. Pressed by circumstances, he had come up with a risky plan, one he soon seemed to abandon, sinking into silence with a look of quiet defeat.

Sitting beside him, Mr. Ba Ngược appeared even more despondent than on the days he claimed to have been "kicked by the horse." He pressed his lips together, his brow furrowed deep in thought, searching for a way out, for both Mr. Bảy and himself. As hard as times were, it was still better to have a functioning Taxi to drive around in search of passengers than to sit staring at a heap of metal, wondering how to feed the family.

Backed into a corner, people often resort to desperate measures. Mr. Ba Ngược suddenly leaned over, tapped Mr. Bảy's shoulder, and suggested in a hushed voice:

"Let me go buy some shaved ice for those two Rê brothers, just to keep them distracted. While they're busy eating, Tuất can slip in and grab our toolbox."

Mr. Bảy looked at Tuất with probing eyes, placing all his remaining hopes on the apprentice he had come to regard as a nephew over the past few months. Tuất nodded without hesitation.

Everyone at Mr. Bảy's garage knew about the Rê brothers' fondness for shaved ice, a city treat utterly foreign to their remote highland village. The first time they encountered it was when they saw Tuất enjoying a cup near the garage. The brothers usually spent their days wandering around Mr. Hai Sang's garden, rarely venturing beyond the patch of grass in front of the house. One afternoon, they spotted Tuất nearby, tilting his head back to savor a spoonful of shaved ice glistening with red syrup. The two stood frozen, their lips moistened with longing. Moved by sympathy, Tuất led them to a vendor at the end of the alley and treated them to their very first cups. Since then, the other mechanics would occasionally do the same, offering the brothers this exotic refreshment as a small gesture of kindness.

This time, while Rê and Ri accompanied Mr. Ba Ngược to buy shaved ice, Tuất slipped quietly into Mr. Hai Sang's garden. The dogs, once known for their ferocity, recognized him and wagged their tails with delight. They remembered him from the times he had played soccer with the Rê brothers near the gate, and no longer saw him as a stranger.

Tuất walked directly toward the family's private garage. Mr. Hai Sang's brown Mercedes wasn't there, only Mrs. Hai's green car sat in the shade. That confirmed what Mr. Ba Ngược had said: Mr. Tư had likely driven Mr. Hai Sang and his wife out in the morning.

As Tuất ventured deeper into Mr. Hai Sang's private garage, he spotted Uncle Bảy's steel toolbox lying on the cement floor against the wall. Without hesitation, he picked up the familiar box and made for the gate. But just before he could reach it, the sharp honk of Mr. Hai Sang's car pierced the air outside. Startled by the sound, Rê dropped his piece of shaved ice to the ground and darted across the street to open the gate.

Suddenly, Tuất found himself face-to-face with Mr. Hai Sang's car. Panic surged through him. He dropped the toolbox and bolted out the gate as fast as his legs could carry him. Mr. Hai Sang, recognizing the boy, shouted for the Rê brothers to give chase. They obeyed, sprinting after Tuất down a narrow alley, but soon turned back, hesitant to stray too far from home and risk getting lost.

Tuất, however, knew there was no turning back. He pressed on, weaving through one alley after another. Though unfamiliar with the surroundings, he had a rough sense of direction and moved with urgency, determined to put as much distance as possible between himself and Mr. Hai Sang's house. After several glances over his shoulder confirmed that no one was following, a wave of relief washed over him. He slowed his pace and began making his way toward the din of traffic, car horns and engine roars guiding him back to the road.

As Tuất emerged onto Hậu Giang Street, the main artery connecting Saigon to the Mekong Delta, he was startled by the unusual bustle.

The lanes were choked with cars, motorbikes, bicycles, and a flood of pedestrians, all moving in the same direction, surging from the outskirts into the city. The usually vibrant shops stood oddly quiet. Apart from a few scattered groups, people simply stood along the sidewalks, watching the steady flow of traffic with puzzled, uneasy expressions.

The scene reminded Tuất of the recent conversations between Mr. Sáu 'Navigator' and Teacher Chín about military tensions. A troubling thought crept in: Was South Vietnam about to collapse? Instinctively, he considered returning to his hometown for safety, but it was clearly too late - there were no buses heading in the opposite direction.

Instead, he made his way to the Nguyễn Hoàng residential area in search of Uncle Eight, who lived near the headquarters of the International Commission for Supervision and Control, the body supposedly tasked with maintaining the ceasefire relating to the Geneva Accords of 1954. Yet no one could say what exactly the commission had been supervising for the past twenty years, as the conflict had only deepened, now pressing at Saigon's doorstep.

When Tuất knocked on the door of his uncle's house, he was met by Mrs. Ba, the housekeeper. A few years earlier, after American troops began pulling out of Vietnam, the economy in many provinces, especially those around former U.S. military bases, had faltered. Jobs became scarce, and countless families migrated to Saigon in search of work. Mrs. Ba had been among them. Tuất asked:

"Mrs. Ba, do you know where Uncle Eight is?" Tuất asked.

"I'm not sure," she replied. "The whole family moved out early this morning."

Surprised, Tuất pressed, "What do you mean the whole family moved out? Did they take their furniture?"

"No, everything's still here. They just packed a few suitcases and left. Oddly enough, they gave me the house keys to hold onto - first time that's ever happened. I don't know what's going on, but something feels different this time."

Tuất's mind raced. Could his uncle have gone into hiding? Perhaps even returned to their hometown in Long Xuyên? He asked urgently, "Do you know where they were heading?"

Mrs. Ba frowned, searching her memory. After a pause, she said, "I heard Mr. Châu urging them to hurry. He kept saying they had to get to Admiral Đô's palace before it was too late. There were already many people waiting, and if they didn't arrive in time, the ship might leave without them."

Tuất grew increasingly anxious, unable to make sense of Mrs. Ba's words. The "Mr. Châu" she had mentioned was Uncle Eight's eldest son, a naval lieutenant. But why would he bring the entire family to the Admiral's palace? Troubled by the thought, Tuất turned to Mrs. Ba and asked, "Why was Châu at home? He's on leave?"

She responded quickly, "It didn't seem like a regular leave. This morning, while the family was still having breakfast, Mr. Châu suddenly showed up, urging the elders and the two girls to pack immediately and leave. The elders seemed to know where they were headed, but I wasn't told anything."

Just then, a commotion stirred outside in the front yard of the residential block. Tuất heard someone shout, "Do you know where everyone's going?"

Another voice answered, "I heard some are heading to the U.S. Embassy. Others are rushing toward Bạch Đằng Wharf."

Tuất didn't fully understand why the crowd was moving toward the docks, but something told him it was connected to Uncle Eight's sudden departure. Glancing around the front garden, he spotted a bicycle leaning against the grinding-stone bench. Without hesitation he took it and pedaled toward the wharf, hoping that, by some stroke of luck, he might find his uncle there.

Upon arriving at the Bạch Đằng wharf, Tuất was met with a scene beyond anything he had imagined. Crowds of people, young and old, were scrambling aboard ships moored along the docks. A wave of anxiety surged through him as he took in the chaos, uncertain what danger had driven his uncle's family, and so many others, to flee in such haste.

Nearby, two men stood facing the city, speaking anxiously to each other.

"Where can we find mechanics at this hour?"

"Even if we do, would they make it in time?"

Without hesitation, Tuất stepped forward.

"I'm a mechanic," he said.

The men turned to look at him. Noticing his faded yellow-white shirt streaked with oil stains, their expressions shifted from doubt to cautious hope. One of them asked, carefully:

"Do you know how to fix diesel engines?"

It was an important distinction - diesel engines operated differently from the gasoline engines found in most cars. Though Tuất had worked as a car mechanic, the men weren't sure if he could handle the complexities of a ship's engine.

As Tuất looked around, he couldn't quite grasp the scale of the unfolding disaster, but whatever it was, he knew one thing: if people were fleeing, he didn't want to be left behind. A sudden memory flashed through his mind - Mr. Sáu '*Navigator*' once explaining the workings of diesel engines to him. Gathering his nerve, Tuất responded:

"I know a little about diesel engines."

"What exactly do you know?" one of the men asked.

"Diesel engines are similar to gasoline ones, but they don't use spark plugs. They compress air until it's hot, then inject fuel, which ignites automatically... Sometimes older engines misfire if the fuel isn't injected at the right moment, or if the air-fuel mixture isn't right, they won't start properly either."

Tuất trailed off, suddenly aware that he was speaking at the edge of his knowledge. Everything he had just said came from the few lessons Mr. Sáu had shared. If they pressed him further, he wasn't sure he could keep up the act.

The two men exchanged a glance. Then, after a short pause, one of them said, "Let's get him on board and see what he can do."

With that, the decision was made. Tuất followed them onto the ship, unaware he was stepping into a moment no one could have foreseen. Guided more by instinct than expertise, he began tinkering with the diesel engine, and miraculously, it roared to life. Whether it was luck or fate, that spark of success carried him across an invisible threshold. From that moment on, he was no longer just a boy adrift in the chaos of his time. He was becoming something else: one of the earliest "boat people," as the world would later call them.

Drifting away from the waters off Vũng Tàu, the infamous southern port city less than 100 kilometers from Saigon, they were eventually rescued by a U.S. Navy ship. Their journey led them through a chain of military camps scattered across the Pacific, from the Philippines to islands like Guam and Wake, before finally reaching Camp Pendleton on Californian soil, more than 12,000 kilometers from Uncle Bảy's garage.

This abrupt dislocation marked not only a turning point in their own lives but a seismic shift in the history of an entire nation. The change was so vast that Tuất and his fellow "boat people" could hardly comprehend its magnitude. They drifted through it like sleepwalkers - the past dissolving behind them, the present suspended in limbo, and the future looming as a distant haze on the horizon.

In makeshift shelters, thoughts of the unknown filled their waking hours. The elders quietly contemplated adjusting their ages to improve their chances of finding work in the new land. The younger ones wondered how, and when, they might resume the schooling interrupted by war.

The days unfolded in a monotony of waiting, each one indistinguishable from the next. Yet what they were waiting for - interviews, visas, sponsorship, a path out of the camps - remained uncertain. These unfamiliar words, rarely heard in their previous lives and even more rarely spoken, now hung in the air like foreign incantations, wrapped in layers of ambiguity and shrouded in the fog of a world not yet their own.

Then, one morning beneath a clear sky, news arrived like a breeze of change. Officers from the Canadian Immigration Office had come to the camp. Asylum seekers formed a line, clutching their hopes for approval to resettle in Canada. Tuất was among the fortunate ones whose wish was granted.

While some hesitated, unwilling to face Canada's harsh winters and preferring to wait for an opportunity to settle in the United States, many others were eager to escape the uncertainty and disorder of life in the asylum camps. Families with children grew increasingly anxious, desperate to avoid further disruption to their children's education. For some, Canada's bilingualism offered a measure of comfort. The use of French, in particular, provided older refugees with a sense of familiarity. Despite America's decades-long presence in Vietnam, American English remained foreign to many of them. With French, at least, they could still manage a few phrases, 'Bonjour', 'Merci', 'Au revoir', and feel, if only briefly, understood.

For Tuất, the choice of Canada as his new homeland was, in part, a decision of the heart. Among all the resettlement options, he had been captivated by the image of vibrant red tulips blooming beneath a clear blue sky, a scene prominently featured on posters displayed by a Canadian Immigration Officer at the camp. To him, the flowers seemed to wave in welcome, like a quiet promise of peace after chaos. What he didn't yet realize was that those radiant blossoms were nature's reward after long, punishing winters, a fitting metaphor for the journey he was about to begin on the vast continent of the Americas.

5. The New World

The Americas have long been referred to as the "New World," a name popularized after Christopher Columbus's arrival at the end of the 15th century. Yet centuries before him, Norse explorers from Scandinavia had already crossed the Atlantic and set foot on North American shores. Still, these so-called "discoveries" overlooked a deeper truth: the land was never empty. For thousands of years, Indigenous peoples had lived, thrived, and shaped rich, diverse cultures across the continent - most likely descendants of early migrants from Asia. Ironically, it was these very peoples whom Columbus mistakenly labeled "Indians," believing he had reached the shores of India, half a world away.

Ironically, though latecomers to this land, the Vietnamese refugees might well be called explorers of the New World, for everything here was unfamiliar, full of discovery. Unlike Columbus, who famously mistook the Indigenous peoples he encountered for Indians from the Far East, Tuất and the wave of Vietnamese refugees arriving with him stepped into a world that was not only geographically new but also socially vibrant and diverse. Here, they had the rare opportunity to meet and befriend people from every corner of the globe, each bearing their own stories of loss, resilience, and hope.

One of the first Canadians Tuất and his group of Vietnamese immigrants met upon arriving in Winnipeg was Ramon, a warm-hearted man in his early forties originally from the Philippines. His skin was dark, and his curly hair clung close to his scalp, forming a horseshoe pattern that left a small bald patch at the crown. His round, open face was lit by a constant expression of curiosity, his gaze often reaching out before his words, as if offering a silent welcome. To the Vietnamese residents, Ramon might as well have been one of their own. And in many ways, he was, for always being there when they needed him, always caring, and never failing to see himself as part of their extended refugee family.

Ramon and several Vietnamese refugees shared a large Victorian-style house built in the previous century. The house had four floors, each occupied by different groups. Tuất stayed in a room on the third floor with two former Special Forces soldiers, nicknamed "The Frogs." The second floor was home to Mr. Nhân's extended family, five members in total. The fourth floor was occupied by four young Vietnamese sailors. Ramon, along with his wife and two children, the only non-Vietnamese family in the house, had settled on the ground floor several years earlier.

Before the Vietnamese refugees arrived, Ramon had already learned about them by speaking with the volunteers who regularly visited the house to prepare the rooms. He eagerly awaited their arrival. The day after Mr. Nhân's family moved in, Ramon appeared at their door with a plate of pastries in hand and knocked hesitantly. No one in Mr. Nhân's family spoke English, and Ramon didn't speak Vietnamese, but that didn't matter. They smiled, exchanged gestures, and spent a warm, quiet evening enjoying each other's company.

Seeing someone arrive with what looked like a birthday cake, Mr. and Mrs. Nhân warmly invited him inside. Following the custom from their homeland, they asked their eldest daughter to brew some tea for the guest. But as soon as he called for her, Mr. Nhân suddenly realized that although the Immigration Office had thoughtfully arranged a fully furnished living space for his family, there was no tea in the house.

The Canadian government had covered two months' rent in advance for Mr. Nhân's family, and they were also receiving a monthly allowance of $250 for groceries and basic necessities. Their clothes, though second-hand, had arrived neatly packed in two large cardboard boxes, each nearly the size of a refrigerator. Inside were garments sorted by gender and size, with enough variety for everyone in the family to find something appropriate, even stylish. Just the day before, Beth, a kind-hearted volunteer, had taken them to the supermarket for their first grocery run. But in the whirlwind of resettlement, no one had thought to buy tea.

Feeling obligated to offer his guest something, Mr. Nhân came up with the idea of serving boiled water, worried that cold water might upset the guest's stomach. He and his wife then had to explain to Ramon that their hospitality was genuine - that their choice wasn't meant to appear casual or indifferent. First, however, they had to overcome the language barrier. Fortunately, with the help of their 16-year-old daughter Xuân, who had studied English for two months at the refugee camp, the message was eventually conveyed. After a few minutes, Ramon suddenly burst into laughter and exclaimed in Vietnamese, a phrase he had picked up during his two years of service in Vietnam:

"OK Salem, OK Salem!"

With that, Ramon quickly excused himself and left. Mr. Nhân and his family watched him go, unsure of what had just transpired.

Mr. Nhân recognized the phrase "OK Salem" as street slang once used by children who chased after American soldiers on leave in Vietnam, hoping to beg for Salem cigarettes. Over time, it had become a colloquial way to express excitement or agreement among friends. Yet what exactly Ramon meant by saying it remained a mystery to Mr. Nhân.

Just as Mr. Nhân and his family were still wondering about his sudden departure, Ramon returned, carrying a bag of tea from his room. He handed it to Mr. Nhân with a smile. With that, the host family and their guest joyfully gathered to share the welcoming cake. They sat around the only table in the house, sipping tea together. Due to a shortage of chairs, Mr. Nhân's youngest son had to stand beside his sister.

After several earnest attempts to get Xuân to interpret - "What did he say, my child? What did he say?" - the family finally came to understand that Ramon had once worked as a janitor in American military camps in Nha Trang, Pleiku, and Ban Mê Thuột. These place names needed no translation; Ramon remembered and pronounced them with ease, his voice tinged with warmth and clarity. He often repeated them, even though he had stayed in each for only a short time, always with an affectionate tone, one that echoed the nostalgia Vietnamese expatriates often feel when speaking of their own hometowns.

It was this shared sense of memory and belonging that allowed Ramon, despite the language barrier, to quickly become like a member of the Nhân family.

After enjoying the tea and cake, Ramon asked if he could take a look inside Mr. Nhân's refrigerator. When the door swung open, he widened his eyes at the neatly packed shelves, pointing at various items and gesturing animatedly, shaking his head in amazement. Mr. and Mrs. Nhân, puzzled, once again turned to their daughter Xuân: "What is he saying? What is he saying?"

Eventually, through fragmented gestures and intuition, the family pieced together Ramon's meaning. He was surprised that they had only bought expensive food.

Ramon continued waving his arms and feet, animatedly mimicking something none of them could fully grasp, except for one word he kept repeating: "fini."

Mr. Nhân, who knew a little French, tried to interpret.

"Fini? Finished eating?"

Ramon's face lit up. He nodded eagerly, then, to make sure they understood, offered an example. He pointed to the bald spot on his head and said with a grin:

"Chậm chậm… fini."('Slowly finished'!)

To the Vietnamese refugees, Ramon often spoke in a lively mix of Vietnamese, English, and French, languages he had picked up during his time in Vietnam and was now delighted to use again. Perhaps his point, through all the pantomime and multilingual chatter, was simply this: he was slowly going bald! It was his roundabout way of illustrating the word 'fini' - and, more importantly, to suggest that once the family finished the current contents of their fridge, they should let him know. He would then take them to a different market, one where the food was not only more affordable but also more attuned to their tastes.

After three days of adjusting to the unfamiliar Canadian diet, Mr. and Mrs. Nhân could wait no longer. On the weekend, they knocked on Ramon's door to invite him grocery shopping, bringing along their daughter Xuân to help translate.

The first store Ramon took them to was a modest, narrow shop run by second-generation Italian Canadians.

Though Nhân's family may have been among the earliest Vietnamese refugees to arrive in Canada, waves of immigration from all corners of the world had long preceded them. Italian immigrants, for instance, were a prime example. Beyond the early explorers and a handful of settlers who came to North America centuries ago, modern Canadian immigration history records two significant waves of Italian migration. The first occurred before the First World War, and the second followed the economic boom after the Second World War. During this period, many impoverished farmers from southern Italy left their homeland in search of a better future in this land of opportunity.

In recent years, this Italian grocery store has thrived by catering to the culinary preferences of immigrant communities, including many from the Philippines. Canada, with its vast territory and relatively small population, began actively recruiting workers from abroad in the early 1960s. Government recruiters were dispatched to the Philippines with the goal of attracting skilled professionals and laborers - doctors, nurses, and factory workers among them, like Ramon's family. They were encouraged to immigrate and settle in cities like Winnipeg, the capital of Manitoba, a province known for its brutally cold winters and remote location in the heart of the continent.

The moment Ramon led the Nhân family into the Italian grocery store, they froze, silently absorbing the unfamiliar sights around them. It might be an overstatement to say they felt like drowning souls grasping at a lifeline - but not by much. For a fleeting moment, they stood in silence, swept away by the sight of familiar vegetables and ingredients. After months of wandering more than halfway around the world, it was as if they were suddenly back in their homeland.

The ducks and chickens, already plucked and cleaned, were displayed whole, from head to tail, on metal trays, with their innards neatly arranged nearby on an aluminum platter. Drawn by the prices, which were significantly lower than those at the supermarket, Mrs. Nhân quickly stepped forward to buy a chicken. She also requested the head, neck, and even the rump - items her husband favored during his drinking sessions.

Ramon, spotting a bottle of duck blood on display, pointed at it and gave Mr. Nhân a playful wink, an unspoken invitation to share a beer-drinking session later. Mr. Nhân burst out laughing and replied,

"OK, Salem."

Ramon gave a thumbs-up and quickly made his way to the counter to buy two sets of duck innards. This time, no translation from Xuân was needed. Both men clearly understood: that evening, alongside the chicken porridge Mrs. Nhân would prepare, they would enjoy Ramon's duck blood pudding as a savory companion to their drinks.

Suddenly, Mrs. Nhân pointed at a tray of eggs on the shelf and then at the price tag, shaking her head in disapproval. It was clear she thought the eggs were too expensive. Ramon quickly caught on and, laughing, offered an explanation:

"Chíp chíp … chíp chíp."

Xuân stepped in to translate:

"He's saying 'cheap, cheap,' Mom. He means it's a good price."

But Mrs. Nhân, a seasoned homemaker, stood her ground. Though it had only been her first visit to a Canadian supermarket a few days earlier, she still recalled the prices of basic staples - and she was certain that a tray of eggs there had cost only half as much.

Still trying to persuade her, Ramon picked up an egg, pointed inside it, and repeated:

"Chíp chíp … chíp chíp."

That's when Mr. Nhân suddenly caught on and burst out:

"He's saying they're hatched eggs, dear!"

Nhân asked her daughter to tell Ramon that they would buy those next week for another gathering. Ramon quickly responded in Vietnamese:

"Ba mươi ba … ba mươi ba!" (Thirty-three … thirty-three!)

Mrs. Nhân looked puzzled. Her husband chuckled and explained, "We've found a fellow drinker. He still remembers Vietnam's famous Beer 33." Mrs. Nhân simply shook her head and walked over to the cashier.

Standing nearby, Ramon reminded the Italian shop owner to give Mrs. Nhân a free packet of chicken wings, a promotional gift often reserved for Filipino customers. From that day on, no weekend gathering among the Vietnamese compatriots in Winnipeg was complete without a generous dish of wings taking center stage.

6. The English Class

Many individuals and organizations across Canada were moved by the plight of Vietnamese refugees, extending compassionate support to ease their resettlement and help them overcome the challenges of starting anew in a foreign land.

Driven by diligence and ambition, Vietnamese refugees often found employment within just a week or two of arriving in this unfamiliar land, even in roles entirely new to them.

On weekends, in rented apartments scattered across downtown Winnipeg, Vietnamese compatriots would gather. They spread layers of old newspapers across bare wooden floors and sat around sharing modest meals: platters of chicken salad or, more often, chicken wing curry, made possible thanks to the complimentary bags of wings generously provided by the Italian shop owner. A few cans of beer were passed around as they exchanged stories about life in Canada, often colored by the oddities of their new professions.

Some worked in so-called 'high-tech' jobs, wiring dynamos for electric motors. Others, in 'low-tech' roles, wrapped zinc around broom handles destined for household use. The physically strong took up night shifts as security guards at construction sites, while the slighter among them found work on farms catching worms - supplied to companies that produced fishing bait.

Former navy personnel found themselves repairing canoes, while ex-air force members took jobs as general assistants at small aircraft companies. Many of them eagerly awaited the chance to take their pilot's license exams, hoping to become bush pilots - flying cargo to remote northern communities or transporting sportsmen to wilderness areas for fishing and hunting expeditions.

Some former naval officers took up work as glass blowers, quietly biding their time until their English improved enough for them to enroll in university and resume the engineering studies that war had interrupted back home.

For many Vietnamese women, opportunities were more limited. Most found work in garment factories, where they formed friendships with their Filipina coworkers and learned to navigate the challenges of life in a foreign land. Yet, due to differences in immigration status and personal circumstances, there were limits to what they could share or learn from one another.

For most Filipinas in the factories, Winnipeg was a chosen destination, a step on a practical journey to earn money and support children or family members left behind. In contrast, the Vietnamese refugees were more like tropical trees torn from the soil by a sudden storm, cast adrift in the sea, and washed ashore in a cold, distant land. There, in unfamiliar soil and under an alien sky, they had to choose: adapt or perish.

After an initial period of shock and dismay upon confronting the harsh realities of involuntary migration, many refugees swiftly embraced their new circumstances and resolved to turn adversity into opportunity. With quiet determination, they chose to pursue education and start over. This often meant enrolling in evening or weekend English classes while juggling exhausting factory jobs, referred to with bittersweet humor among compatriots as "pulling the plow."

The phrase captured not only the physical strain of factory labor but also the cultural astonishment many felt when encountering the mechanized intensity of work in a capitalist society, where time was rigidly measured in hours and minutes, and productivity was tracked with clinical precision.

Despite the long hours at work and the exhaustion that came with "pulling the plow," many refugees remained committed to their studies, attending evening English classes with admirable perseverance.

In one such class held every Monday night, the native-speaking teacher would routinely ask his 'students' a simple question to encourage conversation: "What did you do over the weekend?"

About a month after the movie 'Jaws' premiered in Winnipeg, many of the refugees went to see it together, drawn by word of mouth that it featured thrilling shark-hunting scenes, entertaining even without full comprehension of the dialogue. When they returned to class the following Monday, they proudly responded in unison, "We watched movie."

The teacher followed up with, "Where did you watch the movie?"

Again, the whole class answered in chorus, "No Ta To."

The teacher paused, frowning slightly, puzzled. Despite living in Winnipeg all his life, he couldn't recall a theater by that name. After asking the question twice more and receiving the same baffling reply, an older student stepped in to clarify:

"No Ta Quan, No Ta Tu."

It was this more detailed attempt at clarification that finally made things click for the English teacher. He raised his hands in realization and exclaimed, "Ah, I see!" Then, with a cheerful and courteous demeanor, perhaps a reflection of his role as an educator, he graciously took the blame, saying, "Why wouldn't I know that?"

To gently guide his adult students toward the correct pronunciation, he carefully enunciated each word: "In downtown, there are two theaters: 'North... Star... One' and 'North... Star... Two.' Last weekend, you watched the movie at 'North Star Two.'"

The class responded in unison, pleased with their own recognition:

"Yes, yes... No Ta Tu."

While this moment may have briefly tested the teacher's patience, in a tolerant and individualistic society like Canada, imperfect language skills seldom posed a serious obstacle to the progress of new immigrants.

Within less than a year, many had moved into more stable and comfortable homes, bought their first cars, and adopted a new rhythm of life - fishing in the evenings during summer and taking short trips on weekends. Their most pressing concern, ensuring a proper education for their children, had also begun to settle into a routine. The road ahead still held many unknowns, but it was undeniably brighter than the days spent wandering from tent to tent, from one refugee camp to another, weighed down by uncertainty and the pain of displacement.

7. Homeland In The Heart

The routine of life as recent immigrants to Canada was beginning to take shape for Tuất and his compatriots. Each weekday, they toiled through the grind - what many in the diaspora referred to, half-jokingly, as "pulling the plow." Beneath that phrase, however, often lay a quiet bitterness, the resignation of someone caught in the cruel turns of fate. Amid the exhaustion of daily labor, one might suddenly catch a glimpse of their own life reflected in a line of poetry or a passage from a classic novel - echoes of the unending rise and fall of human fortune.

The weekend told a different story.

From Friday evening onward, it was as if all burdens were momentarily lifted from their shoulders. The atmosphere within the community softened. People gathered with a lightness in their steps, like swallows weaving spring back into the memory of their homeland. Over glasses of beer, beside plates of finely shredded chicken salad or steaming pots of chicken porridge - its fragrance laced with coriander that evoked the scent of distant fields and gardens - homesick hearts found brief solace.

The dishes varied, but the conversations shared in those early days, when the wounds were still raw, bore the unmistakable ache of longing, for loved ones left behind, for a country once called home.

There were many explanations, arguments, and rationalizations for the disasters that had driven them from their land. But one subject seemed to strike deeper than all the rest. One word that pierced the hearts of many former soldiers like a silent wound:

"**Stateless.**"

It was printed clearly on their visas, a legal designation reflecting their status upon arrival. But to them, whether consciously or not, it meant something far more sacred and sorrowful:

"**Without a Fatherland.**"

This led to a simple yet deeply nuanced question, one with no easy answers and little consensus, even among those who had lived through the same upheaval:

"Have we truly lost our homeland?"

Saying "yes" might not be entirely accurate, for the S-shaped stretch of Vietnamese land still lies proudly along the Pacific's edge. And yet, why did they all carry a shared sense of loss, intangible, profound, and unspoken, yet silently understood, as if something essential had slipped away, perhaps forever?

Still, when the conversation turned toward the demands of daily life in their new surroundings, it often narrowed to a more practical theme: how to resume their education, interrupted by years of war.

The five young naval officers, living one floor above Tuất's, had mapped out a plan: after a year of working and improving their English, they would apply to engineering schools. Meanwhile, three single air force officers, who had previously trained in the United States, had already enrolled at the University of Manitoba. They exchanged advice on filling out application forms, navigating enrollment procedures, and preparing required documents.

One obstacle loomed large: academic records. In the rush to flee, who could have anticipated needing transcripts or diplomas? Under such uncertain and chaotic circumstances, no one had thought to bring

proof of their schooling, yet now, that missing piece could stand in
the way of rebuilding their future.

Sitting among the group - most single, a few married with children -
Tuất listened to their ambitions of continuing their studies in Canada.
Their resolve fanned the embers of his own unfinished education, and
a sharp regret pierced him for having once brushed aside his parents'
advice, now echoing in his mind:

'Rừng 'nhu' bể thánh khôn dò,
Nhỏ mà không học, lớn mò sao ra.'

(The forest of scholars' wisdom and the ocean of sacred learning are
unfathomable; if one does not delve into them when young, how can
one hope to navigate them later in life?)

8. Tuất's First Job

Tuất's migration journey was no exception to the broader experience of Vietnamese refugees striving to rebuild their lives in a foreign land. Like many others, he endured the initial turbulence of displacement with quiet resilience, gradually adapting to a world that often felt alien yet full of promise. His path mirrored the shared spirit of survival, but it wouldn't be an exaggeration to say it also took on some peculiar twists of its own, occasionally veering off into the less-traveled (and sometimes downright unexpected) terrain.

Though he was fortunate to be welcomed by a warmhearted and dedicated group of sponsors who did their best to make him feel at home, that kindness alone could not shield him from the culture shocks woven into daily life, nor from the ache of homesickness that settled deep within. In those early days of discovery and disorientation, when every small encounter became both a lesson in adaptation and a quiet reminder of what he had left behind.

Tuất was sponsored by a group of workers from the Whiteshell Nuclear Research Establishment, located about 100 kilometers northeast of Winnipeg.

Alek, a physicist, took the lead on behalf of his volunteer colleagues. He maintained regular contact with immigration officers and the Red Cross, striving to understand the specific needs of refugees so their assistance could be as effective and respectful as possible. Driven by sincere curiosity and care, he also made an effort to learn about Vietnamese customs and traditions, scouring books, newspapers, and documents from Winnipeg's central library. If one were to measure the depth of his compassion, it might be found not in words but in the hundreds of kilometers he willingly drove each weekend. He and his fellow volunteers lived in Pinawa, a secluded 'company town' nestled in the woods near the research facility where they worked.

While awaiting Tuất's arrival in Canada, Alek took it upon himself to prepare the essentials for his new friend's arrival. Aware that Tuất was coming from a tropical climate and would soon face the unforgiving cold of Manitoba, where winter temperatures could plummet to minus forty degrees, Alek made it a priority to buy two thick blankets and a parka, the kind of heavy, hooded coat traditionally worn by Inuit to brave the Arctic chill.

One day, while digging through various cultural materials, Alek stumbled upon a curious detail in a CIA research report: Vietnamese people relied heavily on fish sauce as a primary source of protein and bone nutrients, especially given their limited milk consumption. Alarmed at the idea of Tuất going without such a crucial staple, Alek dashed off to a nearby Chinese grocery store, but came up empty-handed. After a few inquiries, he learned that he needed to visit a Filipino market instead. There, he triumphantly secured two precious bottles of Thai fish sauce, which he treated with reverence, practically cradling them like rare artifacts. The next day at work, he proudly paraded the bottles around the lab, showing them off to every colleague who would listen.

Whenever Alek stumbled upon intriguing tidbits about Vietnamese history, culture, or customs, he eagerly shared them with his colleagues during lunch breaks in the company cafeteria. One day, he appeared particularly surprised, almost incredulous, after reading a document that claimed the Vietnamese lowlands had no traditional folk dances of their own. According to the source, all of Vietnam's traditional dances originated from the highland communities in the mountainous regions.

Equally fascinating to Alek was a linguistic study speculating on the origins of the Vietnamese people. The study suggested that the Vietnamese may have migrated inland from coastal or island regions, based on the linguistic similarities between Vietnamese and several Austronesian languages. For instance, when a Vietnamese person calls a swimming creature 'cá' (fish), it echoes the 'ikan' of Malay and Indonesian, or 'i'a' in Samoan and Hawaiian.

After hearing Alek recount the story, Tuất couldn't help but wonder: Could this newfound understanding shed light on the ancient Vietnamese legend of being descended from the Dragon and the Fairy - the dragon of the sea and the fairy of the mountains? Perhaps, he mused, it hinted at a time when seafaring peoples drifted into the Red River Delta and some venturing inland toward the mountains, while others returning to the sea.

Thanks to Alek's attentive care and the wholehearted support of his volunteer group, Tuất felt less disoriented than many of his fellow countrymen in similar circumstances. Yet, true to the pioneering spirit of North American settlers, Alek believed in empowering others rather than offering daily handouts. He subscribed to the philosophy of lending someone a fishing rod so they could catch their own fish - or even renting one out, if that better suited their entrepreneurial drive, but never simply handing out fish day after day.

Thus, even though Tuất was well cared for during his first days in this new land, he, like many others, still had to shoulder the burden of building his own future. While waiting for the immigration officer to find a mechanic job that matched his experience, Tuất took on various odd jobs that the officer could arrange.

At one point, he accepted a temporary position catching worms on a bait farm at the city's outskirts. The job itself struck him as unusual - back in his homeland, no one raised worms, let alone hired people to collect, box, weigh, and sell them. But even that wasn't the strangest thing he encountered there.

Besides worms, the farm owner kept several dairy cows. One newly purchased cow was yielding far less milk than expected, so the owner brought in a veterinarian. Having spent his youth herding buffalo by day and smoking out mosquitoes for them at night, Tuất had never imagined a doctor for cattle. During the lunch break, his curiosity wouldn't let him miss the chance to watch.

To his surprise, the veterinarian, wearing the same crisp white coat as a physician for human, began by moving a compass slowly across the cow's belly, discussing the findings with the owner in terms no bystander understood. The other laborers were just as puzzled. Eventually, a young co-worker from a nearby farm offered an explanation.

While grazing, cows can inadvertently ingest stray metal - nails, bits of fence wire, and other debris scattered across the pasture. These sharp fragments may travel through the digestive tract, injuring tissue, causing discomfort, and ultimately reducing milk production. To prevent such harm, farmers have the cow swallow a finger-sized magnet, which settles in the stomach and attracts any ingested metal. By sweeping a compass across the cow's abdomen, a veterinarian can confirm whether this "magnetic therapy" is in place: a deflected needle signals that the magnet is doing its job.

As curious as it sounded, Tuất was excited to receive a call from the immigration officer confirming that the hardware store's service garage had accepted him as an apprentice. He had been counting down the hours. Word was that a mechanic's pay far exceeded the meager $2.25 he earned from temporary odd jobs - just enough to scrape by on food, rent, and bus fare. Even at apprentice wages, he would earn nearly double that. "Plenty left to buy gifts for the family," he thought.

Though he still had no way to contact his village, Tuất never stopped imagining the presents he would send home. Every time he browsed the aisles of a store, where almost everything seemed novel and wondrous, he pictured surprises for the loved ones he missed: a soft white towel for his mother, a gleaming Zippo lighter for his father, packets of ginseng tea and boxes of tonic for his grandmother.

And, at last, the chance had arrived. As the first light of dawn brushed the city streets, Tuất buttoned his only clean shirt, slipped the bus fare into his pocket, and stepped outside. He was on his way to the garage - a world he knew by heart. He felt ready to begin the work he had longed for, to carve out a new chapter in his life.

Soon, a routine took shape. Twice a day, Tuất changed buses at the stop on the city's main boulevard, directly in front of a jewelry store. While he waited, his feet would drift, like a loyal little dog, pulling his unseeing heart toward the window. He stands motionless, staring through the glass as his soul drifts after the diamonds that glimmer like stars above a trellis of fresh melons. Not long ago, though it feels like centuries, a breeze lifted a curtain of dark hair beside the whetstone. In one fluid motion she tucked a stray strand behind her ear, a gesture still graceful and discreet, exposing a shy earlobe that seemed to appear on a dare, as if waiting to be adorned with pearl or jade. Whenever Tuất looks at the earrings in the glass case, he yearns to possess them, though for whom he cannot say. No one knows, and no one asks.

9. Weekends Awaited

Saturday arrives, as it always does, carrying its quiet promise of delight. Since Friday afternoon a bright current of anticipation has been rising in Tuất, but it must wait until the five-o'clock strike releases him from the factory floor. Only then does his heart grow light, like a child's balloon slipping free, sailing into whatever sky the day allows: pewter with rain, bitter with snow, or serenely blue. Weather is irrelevant.

His pulse hums, like a caged bird testing its wings, eager to fly until fatigue forces it earthward in search of sustenance. What to eat, where to eat, and how long to linger, these choices belong solely to him. When hunger speaks, he may claim an entire submarine sandwich from the corner shop favored by the young and the beautiful. There, sandwich in hand, he watches the restless stream of pedestrians hurry past, bound for destinations he cannot guess. Their fleeting presence reassures him that in this wide world he is not, after all, alone.

When he craves something dirt-cheap, Tuất heads to "Mc Đồ Nợ", the wry nickname his compatriots have pinned on McDonald's. There, a hamburger and a paper cup of Coca-Cola cost him barely a dollar. On evenings when he feels like "fine dining," he strolls to the "Silver-Haired Old Man," their playful label for Colonel Sanders's Kentucky Fried Chicken, and splurges on a box of crispy wings. Sitting there, nibbling, he lets the faint echo of Eastern spices hitch him a ride back toward his hometown, if only in memory. The stop is practical, too: the restaurant shares a wall with the supermarket, so once he's finished eating he need walk only a few steps to pick up groceries for the week ahead.

Most families spend Saturday morning at the market, but Tuất prefers to keep his weekend wide open, ready to accept any spur-of-the-moment invitation from fellow compatriots - whether for a quick drink, an impromptu fishing trip, a leisurely walk in the park, or a dash to some scenic lookout. He has learned that such unplanned adventures rarely disappoint, and after five days of speaking little Vietnamese on the factory floor, even a brief Saturday conversation in his mother tongue lifts his spirits.

This day, though, his phone stays obstinately silent. He was up at dawn, lugging two baskets of laundry to the coin-op, and now he wonders if any calls slipped past while the machines rumbled. No matter. Tonight he is bound for Ramon's "surprise party," whatever that may entail, and he knows one thing for certain: he had better dress sharp - someone important awaits him there.

Alone in his apartment, Tuất had just finished ironing his favorite outfit: a pair of nearly new, slightly loose jeans gifted by the church, and a pink long-sleeved shirt. He loved the shirt not only because it broke the monotony of the colonial-era whites that still masqueraded as propriety, but also because its vibrancy matched his buoyant weekend mood.

He planned to iron the rest of the laundry when a knock echoed through the apartment. Still gripping the iron, he heard Mr. Long call out:

"Tuất, come up for drinks!"

Wrestling his feet into the oversized leather slippers, another church donation, he shuffled to the door. Mr. Long was already leaning over the upstairs banister.

"And bring your cup!" he added.

Upstairs, the four naval "brothers" have little more than a single rice bowl apiece, and between them they share only two communal dishes for fish sauce and other condiments.

Tuất hesitated, unsure what to say. The previous afternoon, on his way home from work, he had run into Ramon, leaning against the porch rail, cigarette in hand, keeping an eye on his son playing on the sidewalk with a cluster of neighborhood children. Ramon had cheerfully invited Tuất to join the family gathering this day, and Tuất had accepted with equal good cheer. Still, eating with outsiders, even someone as warm-hearted as Ramon, was never quite the same as sharing a meal with one's own "brothers," especially when those brothers would surely be bringing their customary drinks.

Tuất was still wavering, Mr. Long's invitation unanswered on his lips, when heavy footsteps thundered up the stairs from the floor below. It was Mr. Nhân. Catching sight of Tuất lingering in the doorway, he slipped an arm through his and laughed:

"Nothing beats heading upstairs for a drink, my friend, does it?"

Not wanting to disappoint him, Tuất nodded. He ducked into his room for his rice bowl, then followed Nhân up to the sailors' floor.

Even before the door swung open, the rich scent of curry spilled into the corridor - a fragrant tide that lifted every exile's heart and swept it back to remembrance feasts in distant villages. Inside, the living room was almost bare, furnished only with sheets of newspaper carefully layered across the hardwood to serve as makeshift dining mats. From the kitchen, Quốc emerged cradling the steaming pot and placed it at the centre on an extra-thick stack of newsprint - insurance against another scorch mark like the one that had recently drawn the landlord's ire.

Here, a daily paper runs to forty-odd pages, more than enough to repurpose as table mats. In Vietnam, by contrast, a mere four pages once sufficed for an entire readership.

Yet within those slender sheets of a Vietnamese newspaper, lay something for everyone. The curious scanned the front page for the latest headlines. The intelligentsia lingered over editorials and opinion pieces, weighing trenchant commentary on world affairs or laughing till tears flowed when Chu Tử's 'Pond of Ducks' exposed life's absurdities. Children raced to page three for the Monkey King's gravity-defying escapades in the comic strips. Teenagers lost themselves in the melodrama of Duyên Anh's 'Velvet-Eyed Loan', or stole glances toward the back to savor the whispered intrigues of Lê Xuyên's 'Village Chief's Wife'. Women, young and old, whether burdened by unspoken sorrows or simply curious, found solace in Mrs. Tùng Long's advice column, 'Untangling the Threads of the Heart'. Men read it, too, though furtively, afraid of teasing or being thought overly sentimental.

The 'brothers' settled on the hardwood floor as Long cracked open a bottle of beer and filled their glasses. Nhân grinned in approval.

"Chicken curry and beer - who could ask for more?"

Ever since they'd discovered their Italian store owner's bargain chicken-wing specials, no get-together was complete without wings: grilled, fried, even boiled, and invariably simmered in curry. Tonight, however, Quốc broke with tradition.

"There's a curry even better than wings, Nhân," he announced.

Nhân arched an inquisitive brow. Minh chuckled, lifting his glass.

"Let's eat first," he said. "You can decode the secret later."

Quốc ladled steaming curry into two bowls while Phúc handed out thick slices of bread. Nhân's eyes widened.

"French baguette, too? Now that's authentic."

Earlier in the day, Phúc had spent more than an hour on two buses to Saint-Boniface, the city's French quarter, just to fetch those crusty loaves. Perhaps he was chasing the taste of childhood breakfasts; or perhaps, after so much upheaval, he simply craved the small comfort of something familiar and within reach.

Nhân tore off a chunk of baguette, swept it through the curry, and took a slow, deliberate bite. Brows knit, he gazed at the ceiling as if searching for clues in the plaster.

"Hmm… smells like wild game," he murmured.

The four navy brothers burst out laughing. Minh clapped him on the back.

 "Sharp palate, big brother."

"It's Quốc's porcupine curry," Phúc explained. "Go on - give it a real taste."

The dish owed its appearance to pure chance. The day before, while the men were driving beyond the city limits, their car had struck an unlucky porcupine. One passenger, a former soldier skilled at turning camp mishaps into supper, suggested they make the most of fate's bounty. After butchering the animal, he sent half to a neighboring army unit and passed the rest to the navy lads.

Quốc now hoisted the steaming bowl and grinned.

"If a Canadian saw me eating this, he might take off running."

"Not necessarily," Phúc countered. "I read about people in the States who eat worms."

"Worms? Get out of here."

"I'm serious. The magazine showed a guy twirling a forkful of worms like spaghetti - couldn't wait to dig in."

"Another eccentric looking for attention?" Nhân asked.

"No," Phúc replied. "It was a scientific study. A food researcher discovered that earthworms are packed with protein, so he created a worm-salad recipe."

Quốc shook his head. "Americans, always practical and scientific. Still, I couldn't do it. The idea alone makes my skin crawl."

Phúc leaned in, "You don't have to look as far as the States. Right here in Winnipeg, there are people eating cow dung."

"Come on - seriously?" Quốc said.

"I saw it with my own eyes," Phúc insisted.

He described visiting the University of Manitoba during an open-house tour. In the Food Science department, a professor displayed palm-sized, white "cakes" resembling thick crackers. "They were made from cow dung," Phúc said. "The professor announced it matter-of-factly, then snapped off a piece, popped it into his mouth, chewed, swallowed, and grinned while the whole room stared in shock."

Quốc shook his head. "And nobody finds that disgusting?"

"Plenty do," Phúc said. "Everyone watching, from grown-ups to kids, looked queasy. Some pursed their lips; others clenched their teeth and shook their heads, as if someone had made them swallow medicine."

Long frowned. "Then why isn't that dreadful cake on store shelves yet?"

Setting his curry bowl aside, Phúc explained, "It's still experimental. Half these projects never leave the lab. What matters is that people keep researching, testing, and chasing the strange and new. Sometimes it pays off; sometimes it doesn't."

Minh nodded. "Exactly. It may seem useless today, but a few hundred years from now, when the population explodes and farmland disappears, who's to say what we'll be willing to eat?"

Minh took a reflective sip of beer.

"That campus tour opened my eyes," he said. "In a peaceful country, people can accomplish so much."

"They invent new foods too?" Quốc asked.

"Not exactly, what impressed me was something else." Minh passed a piece of bread to Nhân and continued.

"I stopped by the engineering faculty because some of us are thinking of enrolling there. At the Mechanical Engineering exhibits, I paused at every booth to hear students and professors describe their projects. After only a few stops I was astonished; the research they're doing is beyond anything I'd imagined."

"Really?" Nhân said, eyebrows raised.

"Well, maybe it's only new to me."

"So what have they come up with?" he pressed.

Minh set his beer on the floor.

"They were sharing ongoing projects rather than finished inventions, so who knows where they'll lead. The busiest booth demonstrated a three-dimensional imaging technique - students used laser beams to project a four-legged chair that hovered in mid-air. It looked so real I was tempted to reach out and touch it."

Nhân leaned back, genuinely awestruck.

"Impressive! But what's it for?"

Minh shrugged. "I'm not completely sure, but the faculty's chasing plenty of other practical ideas. Take one Japanese exchange student - he's researching how to build houses on the water."

"Floating houses? Why would they do that?" Nhân asked.

"Japan's crowded and land-poor," Minh explained. "So they're eyeing the sea, putting homes just offshore. The clever part is that they plan to harvest the push and pull of tides and waves against the pilings to generate electricity for each house."

"That's fascinating."

"And that wasn't the only eye-opener," Minh went on. "In a joint program with a university in Thailand, they're compressing rice husks and dried coconut shells into clean-burning fuel pellets."

Quốc slapped his thigh. "Brilliant! Vietnam is awash in rice husks and coconut shells. Instead of tossing them out, we could turn them into cooking fuel."

"Exactly," Minh said. "Countries that enjoy peace and stability can pour energy into research and innovation. Think about us, while they were busy in laboratories, we were in uniform, fighting one war after another. Yes, it was for ideals, but it's brutal for a nation to lurch from conflict to conflict: the Trịnh-Nguyễn civil war in the seventeenth century, the fight against French colonization, and now the ideological battles of our own generation."

Long looked at Minh and nodded.

"It's truly remarkable how far they've come. They've poured so much into education and research, thinking not just a generation or two ahead, but sometimes centuries into the future. They were among the first to warn the world about overpopulation, diminishing farmland, and freshwater shortages. Even their proposed solutions sound like science fiction - exploring space, launching satellites, seeking other planets for alternative sources of water or energy."

Phúc gazed out the window, his mind drifting into memory.

"That reminds me of those lines from Trịnh Công Sơn's song 'Đi Tìm Quê Hương' ('Searching for Homeland'):

'Người nô lệ da vàng ngủ quên / ngủ quên trong căn nhà nhỏ / đèn thắp thì mờ....'

(The golden-skinned slaves sleep / Sleep in a small house / The light is dim...)

Long nodded solemnly.

"Absolutely."

Minh gazed out the window with a sigh before shifting the conversation.

"I wonder when we'll finally be able to contact our families," he said.

Nhân shook his head.

"It'll probably be a while."

"Why do you think so?"

"If Vietnam follows the path of the Soviet Union or China, it could take a long time before we can reach anyone back home. Remember what happened in 1949 - after Chiang Kai-shek retreated to Taiwan, Mao Zedong sealed off mainland China almost immediately. Closed all the borders and ports. It's been over twenty-five years since then."

Phúc interjected,

"But in recent years, I've noticed that Mao seems interested in teaming up with the United States to counter Russia."

Nhân nodded thoughtfully before replying,

"Yes, but I'm not sure how far they're really willing to go. It might just be a superficial alliance meant to mislead the Americans. They likely have their own motives."

He lit a cigarette and took a slow puff.

"As for Vietnam, I don't know what to expect. But I hope that if they ever decide to open up, they'll be willing to cooperate with Canada - this country tends to remain neutral."

Phúc added,

"That's why, back at Pendleton camp, some people chose to come here despite knowing how cold Canada is. They were thinking long term. They feared that staying in the U.S. might mean being permanently cut off from Vietnam."

Minh shook his head in frustration.

"Damn it! We might become the true 'stateless' sons."

"Our country is still there, our homeland is still there - it's not like it's disappeared or anything," someone replied.

Phúc smirked, raising an eyebrow.

"When I was in the U.S. for training, I visited a university library packed with Vietnamese literature and history books. So if you're afraid of losing your country, just go there, borrow 'The Tale of Kiều', and read it."

The others turned to Phúc, waiting for an explanation. He took a sip of beer before continuing,

"Don't you remember what Phạm Quỳnh once said?"

Long leaned in.

"What did he say, brother?"

Phúc took another drag of his cigarette, glancing at Long.

"Scholar Phạm Quỳnh was a great admirer of 'The Tale of Kiều' - more than just a fan, really. He saw it as the very soul and essence of our nation. His famous words were: *As long as 'The Tale of Kiều' exists, our language exists. And as long as our language exists, our nation exists...*'"

Long burst into laughter.

"So you mean as long as we still read 'The Tale of Kiều', the country still lives on?"

"Basically, yes - at least within our hearts."

"It's true that a nation's words are important, but what about our flag's colors? The shades of our uniform?"

"That's part of our lives… our youth, to be exact. I don't think we'll ever lose that."

"It'll stay with us - always, in our hearts."

Minh stood up and stretched.

"Well, that's a question for the future. What about tonight? Any plans?"

"Let's go fishing at Lockport!"

Located about 30 kilometers north of the city, Lockport Dam had become a favorite spot for newcomers, thanks to its affordable recreational options, especially fishing. A good catch, like perch or bass, could even shave a few dollars off the weekly grocery bill.

Though absorbed in their conversation - and never one to turn down a chance to hang around with his elder "brothers" - Tuất had reluctantly excused himself. He needed to get ready before heading down to Ramon's apartment.

Quốc spoke up with a hint of regret.

"There's still some chicken wing sour soup left. Stay and finish it, Tuất."

Minh added with a smirk,

"Why waste time on these cheap bites? Something way better's waiting downstairs - a hundred times tastier."

Quốc was more sympathetic.

"I understand, but where else can you find a taste of the homeland like this?"

Long tried to clarify.

"It's not really about the food. They were talking about Ramon's niece."

Quốc looked intrigued.

"Really? I haven't heard anything about that."

Long continued,

"I only heard Minh mention it yesterday. Apparently, Ramon has a niece who works as a seamstress. She arrived in Canada just a few weeks ago as a labor migrant."

Quốc nodded slowly.

"Ah, I see. So you mean he wants to marry her off to Tuất, so she can stay in Canada?"

Tuất quickly brushed it off. "There's nothing like that, brother."

But in his heart, a brief doubt flickered: 'Could that be why Ramon seemed unusually enthusiastic when they met yesterday?' He shook the thought away. Ramon had always been warm and helpful to new arrivals. It would be unfair to read too much into it.

Minh took a sip of beer, gazed out the window, and whispered,

"That's life. Those who seek may never find, and those who've found, never seek."

Phúc understood that Minh was speaking about his own fate. While many, like Ramon's niece, dream of immigrating for a better life, a goal often difficult to attain, Minh and his fellow soldiers had been swept here by a twist of fate, seemingly in the blink of an eye. As Minh's closest friend, Phúc worried about his recurring bouts of melancholy, especially this day, seeing him drink despite the doctor's advice to abstain from alcohol. Hoping to lighten the mood, Phúc gently steered the conversation back to Tuất's potential date.

"I heard she's very beautiful, Tuất."

Tuất hadn't yet met Ramon's niece. Life had become a relentless back-and-forth, like a shuttle weaving through a loom - home on one end, work on the other. Even neighbors in the same building rarely crossed paths. Still, hearing Phúc's comment, though half in jest, sparked a flicker of curiosity. Tuất suddenly found himself looking forward to the dinner at Ramon's house that evening with a renewed sense of anticipation.

10. Culture Shock And Awe

Tuất's early days in this new land were marked not only by the challenges of survival but by a series of subtle cultural shocks - those quiet, curious moments when unfamiliar customs, clothes, or even compliments unsettled his sense of self, reminding him that he was no longer in Vietnam.

In preparation for Ramon's party, Tuất took a quick shower and solemnly put on his clothes, old to others but new to him, hand-me-downs from the church's donation box. He had carefully ironed them earlier that morning. Standing before the bathroom mirror for nearly an hour, he admired the white buttons gleaming down his chest. From top to bottom, then bottom to top, he examined each one with care. Turning to the side, he glanced over his shoulder to check whether the two pleats ran cleanly down the back. The more he looked, the more he appreciated the shirt's crisp fit and its deceptively expensive appearance, even though he knew it wasn't.

The pink color of the shirt brightened the cheerful mood already swelling within him on that leisurely weekend afternoon, regardless of whether it was the lingering compliments about Ramon's beautiful niece that played on loop in his mind. He dabbed a bit of hair oil onto his scalp and began to style his hair, brushing it back and forth, again and again, until the bristles behind his ears lay flat and smooth. In the end, every strand clung so neatly that, as the saying went, "even a fly without a walking stick would slip and fall."

Time passed swiftly, and before he knew it, Tuất was already late for his appointment with Ramon. He hurried down the stairs to the party, where Ramon warmly greeted him and led him straight to the dining table, already laden with plates and glasses. Ramon's wife - whose real name was Mary but was often referred to simply as "Ramon's wife" - brought out a pot of beef stew from the kitchen and placed it at the center of the table.

This was no ordinary stew. Ramon had asked Mary to prepare it using a recipe he had learned from a Vietnamese family he had befriended during his time working in Vietnam. To him, it was an unforgettable dish, one he believed would surely impress Tuất.

And he was right. Tuất gazed at the tender chunks of meat bathed in a rich, red tomato sauce, as if beholding a long-lost treasure. It stirred memories he hadn't felt since the days of living in makeshift tents at American military camps, surviving on bland, unfamiliar meals, except for the occasional bowl of oatmeal. Many had eagerly lined up for that each morning, as it faintly resembled rice porridge.

Now, seated before this hearty stew and treated like royalty, Tuất couldn't help but feel a quiet sense of entitlement creeping in. Suddenly, he found himself wishing for a few spicy chili peppers to accompany Ramon's dish.

The last time Tuất had the pleasure of enjoying beef stew was during a trip with Uncle Bảy, the chief mechanic, to Dầu Giây, about 70 kilometers east of Saigon, to repair the grader of a rice mill owned by Mr. Hai Sang. Since it was the weekend and the children were off school, Mr. Hai Sang brought the whole family along to visit their nearby fruit orchard. Coming from Saigon, just past the old French rubber plantation and on the edge of the forest, you could spot several jackfruit and durian trees in the orchard, not far from the national highway. Behind the farm, a shallow stream marked the boundary between Mr. Hai Sang's five-acre plot and the vast, dense forest. Occasionally, silhouettes of ethnic villagers could be seen darting across the stream, hopping nimbly from stone to stone before vanishing into the foliage.

At lunchtime, the family spread two ponchos on the grass beside a pot of beef stew and a basket of fresh baguettes brought from Saigon. Under the shade of two jackfruit trees, the whole group gathered to eat. Before the meal, Uncle Bảy and Tuất would walk down to the streambank to pick a handful of wild chilies. They were fiery yet fragrant, but not "too harsh," as Uncle Bảy liked to put it. Even with plain rice, they were delicious; but paired with the rich beef stew that Mrs. Hai Sang had cooked herself, they were a true delight.

After each bite of chili, the two would save the stems to count them afterward, competing to see who could handle the most heat. As always, Uncle Bảy emerged the clear winner. Recalling this little memory, Tuất smiled to himself.

Reality set in when Ramon laughed and called out to the kitchen, "The boss is here. Let's start the feast!" Tuất knew he was joking, but he couldn't help finding it amusing to be called "the boss." Ramon's daughter, Alexa, two years younger than Tuất, hurried over and placed a wooden cutting board on the table. On it was a dish of pork stew with fermented shrimp paste, a Filipino specialty, the sauce still gently bubbling.

She was followed by Ramon's niece, carrying two small plates of dipping sauce. She stood across from Tuất, leaning in slightly to place a plate in front of him. From just inches away, she suddenly looked up, her eyes sparkling as they met his. In that fleeting glance, Tuất sensed a greeting, a question, a flicker of affection, a playful challenge, and perhaps even an attempt to hide something deeper.

Typhoon No. 9, predicted to reach level 11 intensity, had just swept across the central coast of Vietnam after forming in the Philippines. Tuất, a young Vietnamese man who had left home at sixteen and once served as a boat captain's assistant navigating turbulent rivers and seas, now found himself in a very different kind of storm, one without wind or rain, yet one that had rocked him just as suddenly and just as deeply.

Once everyone had taken their seats, Ramon formally introduced his niece, who sat across from Tuất. Her name was Charmaine. She had a hint of Western features, most notably her slightly upturned nose. Her face was radiant, like a blooming flower, framed by jet-black hair that cascaded over her shoulders, with a few strands gently brushing her cheeks and swaying in front of her.

Raising a beer bottle to signal the start of the gathering, Ramon turned to Tuất and offered a toast, using one of the few Vietnamese phrases he had picked up:

"Bottoms up!"

Tuất, caught off guard by Ramon's attempt at Vietnamese, chuckled and quickly raised his bottle in return.

"Bottoms up!"

Since the host and guest didn't share a common language, conversation quickly stalled. Still, Ramon, ever the gracious host, generously piled food onto Tuất's plate. Just moments earlier, the dishes had stirred up a wave of nostalgia in Tuất - memories of home, of flavors long missed. He had looked forward to savoring each bite, to quenching the quiet longing within. That was before the storm arrived - before Charmaine's presence across the table disrupted everything.

With her shy demeanor and occasional glances in his direction, Charmaine leaned toward Alexa, whispering something with a mischievous smile. Though subtle, the teasing signals exchanged between them didn't escape Tuất's notice.

He suddenly felt unmoored, torn between the familiar comfort of the food in front of him and the fluttering unrest in his chest. Ramon urged him to eat, then launched into a spirited story - no doubt recounting memories of his time in Vietnam. But Tuất could barely follow. His English was limited, yes, but that wasn't the real problem. What drowned out Ramon's words was the steady, thunderous beating of his own heart.

Still, he caught fragments - familiar names like Nha Trang, Pleiku and Ban Mê Thuột - places Ramon had surely reminisced about many times. Tuất nodded along eagerly, chiming in at the right moments, "Yes, yes - Ban Mê Thuột, Pleiku, Nha Trang," hoping to show he was keeping pace, even if his thoughts were elsewhere.

Ramon seemed to long for Vietnam just as deeply as the Vietnamese expatriates around him. Yet while he fondly reminisced about captivating memories of a faraway place he had once visited, the Vietnamese carried a heavier nostalgia - for familiar, cherished images that had once been an inseparable part of their lives.

After indulging in his own recollections of Vietnam, Ramon turned to Tuất and reintroduced his niece. Seizing the opportunity, Tuất summoned his courage - and his limited English - to greet her:

"Where you from?"

Though the words weren't grammatically perfect, the intent was clear. Charmaine glanced shyly at Alexa, silently asking for help. "Knowing I'm from the Philippines and still asking," she thought, but she answered anyway, with a playful smile:

"Philippines."

The two cousins exchanged another round of giggles. Ramon stepped in to ease the moment, explaining that Charmaine's father was Spanish and her mother a native of Mindanao, where Charmaine was born and raised.

Tuất's eyes lit up at the mention of the name of her birthplace, and he quickly responded:

"Yes, yes! I know, I know."

He smiled to himself, amused. He hadn't expected to hear "Mindanao" - a place he remembered only faintly from a geography lesson in sixth grade. Yet here, sitting across from him, was someone from that very island. It felt oddly delightful, as if the world had suddenly folded in on itself.

Then the atmosphere thickened into silence, broken only by the soft clinking of spoons against plates. Each person drifted into their own private thoughts. Tuất longed to say something to Charmaine, if only to keep the conversation going and spare Ramon from feeling awkward. But his limited English had already been exhausted, and even if he had known more, the words had long lost their wings in the heat of the moment.

Quietly gripping his fork, Tuất found himself murmuring the tune of a folk song in his head:

'Thấy em như thấy mặt trời,

Thấy thời thấy vậy, trao lời khó trao.'

(Seeing you is like seeing the sun; it's there for the eyes to behold, yet exchanging words is so difficult.)

The more he thought about it, the more he admired the wisdom of his ancestors. He had always known that the folk poetry of his homeland was rich - overflowing with metaphors, proverbs, and centuries of lived experience. But now, he couldn't help but marvel that it somehow managed to capture even the full absurdity of his current predicament: a young Vietnamese man, adrift in a foreign land, sitting at a dinner party, unable to say anything meaningful to the girl across the table - all because of a language barrier.

Ramon glanced around and saw that everyone had finished eating. He discreetly signaled to his daughter, and Alexa and Charmaine stood up from the table together, quietly switching off the dining room lights.

Tuất was startled. "Why is there a power outage in Canada? Just like back in Vietnam?" The thought had barely crossed his mind when the lights suddenly flickered back on.

Charmaine returned, gently carrying a plate with a birthday cake and placing it in the center of the table. The entire family broke into the familiar birthday tune, the classic song known across the world.

Except Tuất had never heard it before.

Watching everyone sing with such joy, he tried to follow along, offering a polite smile. But his awkwardness didn't go unnoticed. Ramon and his family exchanged puzzled looks.

"Isn't today a special day for you?" Ramon asked.

Tuất hesitated. "Aside from it being the weekend, what could be so special?" he wondered. Then he replied honestly, "I don't know."

Ramon looked stunned. He asked again, just to be sure:

"Isn't today your birthday?"

Two weeks earlier, while helping Tuất complete a school enrollment form, Ramon had noticed his date of birth.

Only then did it dawn on Tuất. His eyes lit up with sudden realization.

"Yes, yes, today is my birthday," Tuất said, smiling at last. "You're right."

Ramon let out a quiet sigh of relief and gently explained to Tuất that the birthday celebration was for him. He even hinted that the cake had been specially made by Charmaine.

Tuất was speechless. He shook his head in disbelief, unable to accept the overwhelming kindness. It felt unreal, too generous, too unexpected. He couldn't fathom that such warmth was truly meant for him.

It took him a while to come to terms with it. Glancing at each person around the table, he finally managed to stammer, "Thank you," over and over again.

That night, lying awake in his room, Tuất couldn't help but feel a pang of guilt. He worried that he had dampened the joy of Ramon's family, especially disappointing Ramon with his delayed reaction.

The more he thought about the evening, the more he appreciated Ramon's thoughtfulness. Trying to console himself, he murmured in the quiet of his room:

"Since the day I was born, no one has ever reminded me of my birthday. So how could I have remembered it myself?"

Except for his very first birthday, celebrated out of tradition, Tuất had no memory of any birthday ever being acknowledged. His maternal grandmother, however, often recounted that day to relatives near and far. At a solemn ceremony marking the first year of life, it was customary to present the child with three symbolic objects, each representing a possible future. The item the baby chose was believed to reveal a glimpse of their destiny. In Tuất's case, the wooden tray held a pen, a handful of rice, and a mirror. He reached for the mirror. Some relatives playfully teased that he would grow up to be vain, like a woman who admired herself too much. But his grandmother firmly rejected that notion.

"No," she would say, "a mirror means intelligence. This little boy will grow up to be very bright."

And that was the only birthday memory Tuất ever carried.

Even on other festive occasions, like the full-month celebrations for his younger cousins, Tuất wasn't allowed to participate, let alone enjoy the sweet mung bean porridge traditionally served at such gatherings.

"Children shouldn't eat food from those celebrations," his grandmother would say, fearing it might dull their wits.

Out of love and caution, she would buy cornmeal from the market as a substitute for Tuất. That's how he grew up favoring cornmeal over dessert.

The cornmeal came wrapped in banana leaves, folded into the shape of a small boat. He would tear off a piece of the leaf to use as a makeshift spoon. Each bite carried a blend of richness, saltiness, sweetness, and the fragrant aroma of corn and sesame seeds, enough to satisfy his craving for the sweet mung bean porridge he was never allowed to taste.

Tuất lay alone in the empty room, surrounded by walls lined with faded, outdated golden floral wallpaper. At the head of the bed, a tall, ghostly lamp cast a dim, solitary glow. He let his thoughts drift along the path of light on the ceiling, chasing the memory of the moonlight that once kept him company in the open fields of his youth. The light shimmered faintly, stirring fragments of old memories.

Then, a sudden realization struck him - why Ramon's mention of his niece, Charmaine, had felt oddly familiar. The name sounded strikingly similar to that of Tuất's former dream girl: Chimène.

Chimène had entered Tuất's life during his time at Thoại Ngọc Hầu High School, when he was studying under Teacher Chương. At nearly seventy, Teacher Chương had long been retired but was personally invited back to teach Civic Education, as many of the younger teachers had been called away for civic duties.

Tuất liked Teacher Chương - not just because the subject was "too easy," requiring little to no study (after all, one ought to know their civic duties simply by growing up), but for another, more compelling reason.

Every week, Tuất eagerly awaited the class, because in the last fifteen minutes, Teacher Chương would share excerpts from the timeless French play 'Le Cid' by the 17th-century playwright Pierre Corneille.

Teacher Chương was so passionate about 'Le Cid' that, according to him, he could pinpoint the exact page of a verse just by hearing a single line recited. No student ever dared to challenge such a claim. And truly, as they watched him recite entire passages fluently in French - his eyes gleaming with recognition, his head gently nodding before he offered a Vietnamese translation layered with meaning - none doubted his words. The class was entranced.

The play told the tragic tale of a doomed love between Chimène and Don Rodrigue. Fate had driven Don Rodrigue to kill Chimène's father in order to defend his own family's honor. In remorse, he offered his life to Chimène, inviting her to take revenge. Yet she could not bring herself to harm the man she still loved.

Torn between love and filial duty, Chimène faced an agonizing choice. When another man volunteered to avenge her father by killing Don Rodrigue and then marrying her, she agreed. To her, this seemed the only way to fulfill her duty as a daughter. But in her heart, she prayed for Rodrigue's safety. When her suitor returned with a sword stained in blood, Chimène, believing her beloved had been slain, broke down in grief. She begged to be released from the marriage and sought refuge in a convent, hoping to bury her sorrow behind cloistered walls.

Little did she know, Don Rodrigue had won the duel, and spared his rival's life, so that he might still hope to win her hand.

In the deep and poignant romance of Chimène's unwavering love for her beloved, many young hearts in Tuất's class were stirred. Poor Teacher Chương, if only he knew, might have found joy in seeing the 'young flock' experience the first pangs of love. Yet, as an educator, he could not help but feel a tinge of sorrow. The civic lesson he wished to leave imprinted in his students' hearts was not merely about romance, but about patriotism, honor, and responsibility - values powerfully embodied in the latter part of the story he so passionately narrated.

Despite the anguish of a broken heart, Don Rodrigue did not falter when his nation was in peril. He marched to the front lines and faced the enemy with unwavering courage. His valor on the battlefield struck fear into opposing forces, who ultimately bowed to him in reverence, acknowledging his nobility. This, Teacher Chương believed, was the true lesson for the youth: the duty of a citizen to their homeland, the sacred obligation to serve one's country before tending to personal ties, and the shining example of a young man rising to greatness in turbulent times.

Since arriving in Canada, Tuất's nights often begin and end with fragmented, timeless images of his past, scenes from his hometown that linger like echoes in sleep. Tonight is no exception, though it carries the tender remnants of wind and rain left in the wake of the afternoon's Charmaine storm. As the clouds part and the winds die down, the old moon quietly returns, casting a soft glow on the heart-shaped leaves swaying gently on the melon trellis behind Mr. Tư the driver's house. The image of Hoa, standing by the mortar on the porch as Tuất first saw her, reappears - clearer, more vivid than before. Carried by the quiet beauty of the moment, Tuất drifts into a dream.

11. Ice Fishing

After the whirlwind of confusion and surprise at the birthday party - a first brush with the quirks of life in this new land – Tuất senses that another unfamiliar experience is just around the corner.

The night before, Alek called, as he often did just to check in, but this time he had a different reason: he invited Tuất on a weekend ice fishing trip. Tuất was taken aback. 'Fishing? In the middle of winter?' The Filipino and Vietnamese fishermen he knew had all long packed away their gear, patiently waiting for summer's return. During a Manitoba winter, the world outside is frozen in silence, wrapped in bitter cold. Tuất couldn't help but wonder if he'd heard Alek correctly: "Going fishing this weekend?"

Tuất was born and raised among the rivers and waterways of the Mekong Delta, so fishing and shrimp trapping were second nature to him. However, when Alek repeatedly mentioned "ice fishing," Tuất found himself genuinely puzzled. Was Alek truly inviting him to go fishing? In Vietnamese, 'fishing' clearly means 'câu cá', and 'ice' means 'nước đá'. While Tuất's English was far from fluent, he was confident he hadn't misheard, especially after asking Alek several times to confirm. That only deepened his confusion. He began to wonder if this was one of those instances he'd been warned about back in the refugee camp, where understanding English sometimes meant flipping the word order. Could "ice fishing" actually mean 'fishing ice'?

Tuất didn't have to wait long for an answer. A busy week at the car repair shop flew by, and on Saturday morning, right on the dot at 11 a.m., Alek arrived in a pickup truck with his fifteen-year-old son in tow. As Tuất approached the vehicle and reached for the door handle, his eyes caught sight of three fishing rods lying in the back of the truck. "So, it really is fishing," he murmured to himself with a mix of amusement and relief.

Once they were on the highway, the world outside unfolded into a dazzling expanse of white. A narrow ribbon of black asphalt stretched ahead, slicing through the endless snow and guiding them forward. On one side, vast fields lay buried beneath a glistening blanket of snow- cornfields in another season, now rendered unrecognizable. On the other, pine forests stood silent and solemn, their branches bowed under the heavy weight of snow. After just over an hour of steady driving, Alek gently eased off the gas and turned onto a narrow road that led toward Pine Lake.

Tuất had visited Pine Lake a few months earlier during an outing with fellow refugees. The lake lay about four hundred meters from the main road, tucked away behind towering old pines. Dense underbrush and tall trees stretched overhead, their branches interwoven and clinging to one another, as if shielding the lake and deepening its wild, tranquil allure.

It was late autumn then. Aside from the steadfast green of the pines, the foliage had shifted into shades of yellow, purple, and even the deep wine-red of blueberry bushes. Looking closely, one could spot clusters of dark, shriveled berries still clinging to the branches - leftovers, perhaps, from a meal unfinished by a mother bear and her cubs.

The lake's surface was calm, smooth like glass, with a few golden leaves floating serenely atop it. Then, a sudden gust of wind stirred the branches, releasing more leaves that fluttered down and drifted idly across the water. The sight stirred in Tuất's mind a line of poetry, an autumn verse by the famed poet Nguyễn Khuyến, which Mr. Văn, his ninth-grade teacher, had once insisted the class memorize.

'Ao thu lạnh lẽo nước trong veo,

Một chiếc thuyền câu bé tẻo teo.
Sóng biếc theo làn hơi gợn tí,
Lá vàng trước gió sẽ đưa vèo.'

(The autumn pond is cold, the water is clear,
A fishing boat floats, tiny and still.
Azure waves ripple with the breeze,
A golden leaf swiftly carried by the wind.}

Though Pine Lake had no tiny fishing boat, the breeze still coaxed ripples across its surface, and the air was quiet enough to hear the faint rustle of distant leaves.

"Here we are - we've arrived!"

Alek's cheerful voice, tinged with his familiar playfulness, pulled Tuất out of his reverie. The younger Alek tugged down his woolen toque over his golden hair, which shimmered in the light, and sprang out of the truck. Tuất followed, stepping into the snow and scanning the surroundings. There was no sign of water now, no ripple or golden leaf drifting on the lake's surface. Yet, by the placement of the ancient pines on this side and the gentle slope rising on the far shore, Tuất could still picture where the lake lay - buried now under a pristine, endless sea of snow. Wherever the eye turned, it was met with one thing: pure, dazzling white.

Looking back, Tuất noticed Alek and his father unloading something from the truck, not fishing rods, as he had assumed. A closer look revealed what it was: an ice auger. 'So this is what ice fishing is all about,' Tuất thought. A few weeks into winter, the lake had frozen solid beneath its snowy cover, with the ice reaching nearly half a meter thick in some places. And yet, fish still thrived below. To catch them, one simply drilled a hole through the ice, dropped in bait, sometimes all the way down to the lakebed, and waited. The rest was just sitting, chatting, and hoping for a bite.

Fortunately, the ice wasn't too thick that day. In no time, they had drilled three fishing holes scattered across the lake. Alek, ever courteous, let Tuất choose his fishing rod first and gave him a friendly pat on the back, proposing a lighthearted competition to see who could catch the most fish.

The rods were all quite similar - short and slender, almost toy-like. Compared to the thick, towering bamboo rods of his hometown, these looked like nothing more than 'toothpicks', Tuất chuckled to himself. Among the three, two were blue and one was red. Tuất chose a blue one, intentionally leaving the other blue and the red rod for Alek and his father. But just as he reached for his rod and before he could step back, Alek and his son suddenly lunged playfully, wrestling each other for the remaining blue one.

"I first!"

"No, I first!"

The father and son playfully tugged at the fishing rod, each trying to claim the remaining blue one. Tuất watched with amusement as they gently wrestled, laughter echoing across the frozen lake.

'If I had known they liked blue this much, I would've left that rod for them,' Tuất mused.

In the end, Alek relented and handed the rod to his son. Grinning, he walked over to Tuất holding the red rod and offered an explanation. His son, Alek said, wasn't actually after the color - it was the bait on that rod. He believed it was lucky and had helped him catch more fish in the past.

Tuất nodded, beginning to understand. 'So, it wasn't the rod's color - they were competing over the bait,' he thought. As an experienced fisherman himself, Tuất understood the logic immediately.

Back in his hometown, any seasoned angler knew the importance of bait. You chose the bait based on the fish you wanted: earthworms for catfish, tiny frogs for snakehead fish, or moldy rice for gourami. And if you were lucky enough to find an ant nest clinging to a guava tree, you'd knock it down and collect the ant eggs, an irresistible treat for gourami. That was a sure way to earn a hearty dish of fried gourami for dinner. Or, at the very least, a comforting bowl of melon soup with fish, simmered just right.

Tuất glanced down at the end of his fishing line to check for bait. To his surprise, it was already there, but it wasn't what he expected. Instead of a wriggling worm or insect, there hung an artificial lure: a shiny piece of metal shaped like a minnow, with a sharp hook no bigger than a fingertip dangling from its tail.

Tuất was baffled. 'Canadian fish must be blind to bite something like this,' he thought. Not only did the bait look fake, but the hook was blatantly exposed, gleaming and menacing in the pristine white landscape.

Back in his village, no one had even heard of artificial bait, let alone used it. Only live bait would do, and it had to be carefully chosen to match the type of fish they hoped to catch. After hooking it, they'd take an extra step: threading a blade of grass over the hook's point to hide its gleam. Even the act of 'going fishing' was wrapped in superstition. On quiet afternoons, when neighborhood kids wanted to invite one another to fish by the ditches, they spoke in riddles or playful code, never daring to say the word aloud. They believed the fish spirit might overhear - and warn all the fish to stay away!

Curious, Tuất glanced at the bait favored by Alek's son, and was stunned. It was nothing more than a green plastic tube, leaf-colored and toy-like, with bulging frog eyes painted white and dotted black in the center. It looked like something out of a child's playset. But at its tail dangled not one, but three vicious-looking hooks, each angling in a different direction like the talons of a predator. And yet, the fish still took the bait. Unbelievable!

Still marveling at the odd bait, Tuất watched as Alek unfolded his chair and settled by the edge of his fishing hole. With practiced ease, he lowered the lure into the water and declared the competition officially underway. Without hesitation, Alek's son and Tuất scrambled to their own spots, pulled out their chairs, and cast their lines with eager anticipation. Alek sat calmly, gripping his rod, eyes trained on the water.

Then, as if forgetting the competition entirely, he looked up and let his gaze drift across the vast, snow-covered expanse. Not a soul in sight, only silence and the pristine white stretching toward the horizon. Tilting his face toward the sun, he seemed to absorb each ray of warmth directly from its celestial source. With a deep, contented sigh, he exclaimed:

"Excellent. There's nothing better than this."

Just then, his son shouted with glee:

"I got one! I got one!"

'That kid really knows how to fish,' Tuất thought, impressed. The boy had hooked a Northern Pike, a species native to these frigid northern waters. Its meat was known to be delicious, but the fish itself looked prehistoric, with a flattened, rugged head that called to mind a crocodile. Its body was long and tubular, olive green with scattered yellow spots, not unlike a spotted moray eel.

This species of fish was known for its aggression. Alek had once been intimidated by one himself. He recalled a summer fishing trip from a few years back: standing on a rock by the riverbank, casting his bait far into the water, then slowly reeling it in - over and over, lost in thought as he watched the drifting clouds overhead. Cast out… reel in… a soothing, almost meditative rhythm.

Then, without warning, just as the bait neared his feet, a Northern Pike exploded from the water, leaping into the air in hot pursuit. It came so close that Alek flinched, thinking the fish was attacking him. The memory still made him chuckle.

Back at the lake, Alek opened his tackle box and pulled out a long-handled pair of pliers to help his son remove the hook from the fish's mouth, lined with sharp, protruding teeth. After a moment of shared admiration, Alek gently released the catch back into the water, to Tuất's surprise.

They weren't fishing for food. For Alek and his son, this was a sport - a game.

Tuất, watching it all unfold, was amazed. He'd never seen fishing treated like this before. As the fish slipped back into the lake, he felt a quiet pang of regret. 'If that fish were grilled,' he thought, 'it would've been delicious.'

After a few minutes of excitement and restlessness, Alek's son began to feel hungry and called out for food. Everyone pulled their chairs over and gathered around Alek's fishing hole for lunch. From his backpack, Alek handed each person a small paper plate topped with three slices of cheese, a few celery sticks, and a couple of baby carrots no longer than a pinky finger.

A few minutes later, he pulled out a carton of fresh milk for his son, and a bottle of red wine along with two plastic cups for himself and Tuất. Turning to Tuất, Alek squinted and said with a grin, "We need this to keep our bodies warm, not to mention, it goes well with the cheese."

Tuất glanced down at the plate, trying to maintain a polite expression. 'Well,' he thought, 'if this is what people eat, then so can I… but what bland food.' Once again, he felt a quiet pang of regret for the missed chance to have grilled fish, or at the very least, a warm, comforting fish stew.

As they ate, Alek and his son animatedly recounted the suspenseful hockey game they had watched on TV the night before. It was an ice sport where two teams used curved sticks to drive a heavy black disc into the opponent's goal. The puck, no larger than the palm of an adult hand, zipped so quickly across the ice that Tuất found it nearly impossible to follow on screen.

He listened as the father and son relived the game with excitement, still puzzled. He couldn't quite grasp how a game like that could ignite such fervor, and even national pride, in this country.

Looking down at the plate, Tuất spotted an old celery stick he had meant to throw away. Absentmindedly, he picked it up and placed it in his mouth. Crunchy. His gaze drifted upward toward the vast sky, where a lone, tattered cloud was floating in from some far-off place. Really far away.

And then, faint echoes from childhood stirred in his mind:

'Grandma, look. I finished all the rice in my bowl. Not a single grain wasted.'

'Yes, my grandson. You are really good!'

Meanwhile, Alek and his son had shifted topics without Tuất even noticing. They were now engrossed in reminiscing about a deer hunting trip in the nearby forest just a few months earlier.

12. Tết

Having narrowly escaped the final days of Saigon, Tuất, like many of his compatriots, spent months in limbo, passing through a series of makeshift camps, many on former U.S. military bases. By the fall of 1975, he had resettled in Canada. Just a few months later, in January 1976, Tuất and the newly arrived Vietnamese community found themselves preparing to celebrate their first 'Tết', or Vietnamese New Year, in a foreign land.

'Tết' is the most important holiday in Vietnamese culture - a time for family reunions, ancestor veneration, and the renewal of traditions. Rich with symbolic rituals and festive celebrations, it marks the beginning of a new year filled with hopes for prosperity and good fortune.

In Winnipeg, Reverend Swanson, although whose name many Vietnamese found difficult to pronounce, became a beloved figure in the community. With sincere dedication, he helped the refugees organize a 'Tết' celebration in the basement banquet hall of his church. It was there, on Saturday, January 31, 1976 - the Year of the Dragon - that the first overseas Vietnamese New Year was joyfully commemorated by the refugee community.

A week before 'Tết', Hiển drove over to pick up Tuất and Minh for a trip to Chinatown to buy candles and decorations for the 'Tết' altar, hoping to bring a festive atmosphere to the community gathering room. Among the group of refugees, Hiển was one of the first to own a car. He had previously studied telecommunications at the U.S. naval base on Treasure Island in San Francisco Bay, later returning there as an instructor. Thanks to his fluency in English and technical background, he quickly found stable employment upon arriving in Winnipeg. Before long, he had purchased a car and a house, steadily following the well-trodden path of immigrants building a new life in a land full of promise.

As Hiển started the car, Tuất, sitting in the back seat, suddenly tensed and looked around, startled. A familiar melody was playing - one he had heard countless times from the radio at Uncle Bảy's garage, a tune that had vanished along with the world he had left behind. Now, after months of silence, it returned, flowing from the cassette player in the front of Hiển's car. The song was not only familiar to the ear but struck a chord deep within Tuất's heart.

Since Tuất was not yet five years old, his mother fell seriously ill and had no choice but to send him to live with his grandparents. Over the next six months, by what felt like divine mercy, her health gradually improved. During that time, Tuất's grandmother spent countless sleepless nights caring for her first grandchild. Every meal, every diaper change, she tended to with love and devotion, growing deeply attached to him. What grandmother doesn't love her grandchild? Yet in this case, her affection was intertwined with a desire to ease her daughter's burden and allow her time to fully recover. Tuất's parents had no choice but to wait until he was old enough to start school before they could gently reclaim him, using that as a natural reason to bring him back home.

Although Tuất lived with his grandmother for only a few years in early childhood, the memories ran deep - like river water once set in motion, impossible to stop, and like sediments once settled, impossible to dislodge. The fairy tales she told and the lullabies she sang to lull him to sleep continued to circulate through his bloodstream. Their gentle melodies murmured in his subconscious, weaving a sky of enchanted memories across the canvas of his childhood.

In that dreamlike realm lived a girl named Tấm, a gentle and filial soul who had been wronged by a cruel stepmother and killed. Yet she endured, her spirit hidden at the heart of a golden apple, hanging from the boughs of a golden apple tree. One day, an old, lonely woman stood beneath that tree and softly called out, "Golden apple, golden apple, fall into my sack, so this old lady can have a snack." And Tấm answered her wish. The old woman unknowingly carried Tấm home, where, while she was away, the girl would quietly reappear to cook, clean, and tend the house - leaving behind traces of warmth and wonder.

The magical wonders gradually took root in Tuất's young soul. Deep within his subconscious lingered the echoes of another mournful melody - one played by the legendary Thạch Sanh, the brave and kind-hearted woodcutter, strumming his lute in a dark cave where he had been cruelly imprisoned by his treacherous half-brother, who sought to steal the glory of rescuing the lost princess.

Over time, the vivid contrasts in these tales - good and evil, beauty and ugliness, virtue and deceit - reflected through their characters like mirrors. They became the steady beam of a lighthouse, guiding Tuất through the journey of life. These stories nurtured within him a heart attuned to both the celebratory joys and the silent griefs of a homeland.

At first, the verses and melodies were just a tangle of images in the child's mind:

'... *Horse, black horse pulling the golden carriage... The prince adorned his steed with gold and silver trappings... lotus flowers swaying with every step...*'

'... I... Í... I... Heading toward the royal palace, the prince escorted the princess home...'

The words and meanings were unfamiliar, stitched together from scenes he had never truly seen. But to Tuất's heart, they spoke differently. He could taste the sweetness in his grandmother's voice, feel the warmth, the tenderness, the quiet love flowing from her soul. And so, he drifted into sleep, lulled by the soft jingle of bells on the prince's horse, dreaming of pink lotuses swaying in the pond beside his house.

Now, lost on an icy island amid an endless expanse of snow, everything felt unfamiliar. From the clouds above to the branches and blades of grass below, from the voices and laughter inside the workshop to the mechanical hum of vehicles outside - everything seemed foreign to Tuất the mechanic. Then, in the stillness, something warm and deeply familiar surged from the depths of memory. It melted the frozen landscape within him, turning the snow into a stream of sweetness, a cool spring trickling into his ears and gently touching his heart.

The music from Mr. Hiển's cassette player wrapped around him like an embrace. There was no mistaking it: the singing voice of the homeland's beloved 'Sister of the Soldiers' - the very voice Tuất once heard every day on the radio and TV at Uncle Bảy's garage. It was the unmistakable voice of 'The Queen of TV', diva Phương Hồng Quế. To Tuất, that cherished voice felt even more intimate now, carrying the warmth and tenderness of a friend he had once secretly loved and never forgotten.

The car pulled up in front of the grocery store and stopped by the side of the road. Minh raised his hand, signaling to Hiển not to turn off the engine - he wanted to hear the rest of the song Diva Hà Thanh was singing. Reaching into the pocket of his parka, Minh took out a pack of Player cigarettes and offered one to Hiển. They cracked open the car window just enough to let the cigarette smoke drift out, careful not to let the biting cold rush in too quickly.

For a brief moment, it felt as though even sitting in an Eskimo tent at the top of the world couldn't stop the two soldier brothers from revisiting the past - those rare moments during military breaks when they sat by their backpacks, listening to music in the shade of the forest, by the edge of a field, beneath the scorching tropical sun.

Only the magic of music, and it had to be Vietnamese music, held the enchanting power to summon phoenix blossoms in the heart of winter, golden apricot flowers upon fields of snow. It could ease the ache of exile, soothe the sorrow buried deep within the hearts of those cast far from home.

Hà Thanh's singing draped the graceful, classical elegance of the imperial court over the profound depth of the Perfume River and the eternal charm of the Ngự Mountain region. If, in the past, her voice had offered serenity amid chaos, then now it was a lullaby of the homeland - comforting the children lost in the great upheaval of earth and sky, reminding them of the nation's long, unbroken history, stretching far beyond the fleeting tremors of a world in turmoil.

As the music faded, Minh stubbed out his cigarette and gazed out the window, musing,

"Looking back, Phạm Quỳnh was only half right."

Hiển turned to him, waiting for an explanation. Minh continued,

"The other day, while we were having a drink, someone brought up scholar Phạm Quỳnh's famous line, something like, '*As long as 'The Tale of Kiều' endures, so will our nation.*' But today, after listening to Hà Thanh I feel compelled to add: As long as our music endures, so will our nation."

Hiển nodded thoughtfully. After a pause, he said,

"True, very true. Hasn't this music been woven into the lives of our youth over the past couple of generations?"

He wasn't wrong. Through the country's many upheavals, modern Vietnamese music - though a relatively recent creation - had become inseparable from the urban youth, like a shadow following its figure through the decades. More importantly, it had taken root in the hearts of the people, spreading across all walks of life. It overcame not only the country's harsh realities but also the social prejudices once aimed at those who sang for a living.

In the most recent historical periods, the joys and sorrows of the people gave birth to songs - melodies and lyrics that captured a full range of emotions: from tender, romantic odes to love, to stirring anthems of patriotism; from the somber resonance of wartime youth, to the restless search for meaning in this earthly life.

The homeland evoked by the music still lingered in the hearts of the wandering brothers, barely faded, when reality returned - ushered in by the sight of an Asian grocery store standing like an island amid a vast ocean of snow. The three brothers snapped back to the task at hand: preparing for the upcoming Tết celebration. They stepped into the Chinese store to buy two packets of red envelopes for lucky money and some votive candles. As they were leaving, Hiển said,

"Now I've got to buy abalones too."

Tuất looked surprised.

"Why's that, brother?"

"The ladies have been racking their brains for days, not knowing what to cook."

"Well, for Tết, braised pork and pickled vegetables should be enough."

"They're worried the Canadian guests won't like it," Hiển chuckled. "And they're not sure if the neighbors can handle the smell of fish sauce."

"Oh, that makes sense," Tuất said. "Even though I've seen Americans in Vietnam gulp down fish sauce like it's nothing, there are definitely some who scrunch up their noses, unable to stand the smell. So, what do the ladies plan to do?"

"They've agreed that we still need to serve some traditional dishes," Hiển replied. "Besides the usual pickled vegetables and braised pork, they're adding shrimp salad. But they also feel the need to prepare something a bit more elegant for the foreign guests. Fortunately, Aunty Bảy knows how to prepare abalone, so she suggested that."

"Abalone for Tết? That's a first for me."

"As long as it's expensive, it counts," Hiển laughed. "Plus, Father Swanson gave us fifty dollars for the Tết celebration. That's a lot. If we spent it all on braised pork, I'm afraid we wouldn't have enough pots to hold it!"

"Yeah," Tuất agreed, smiling. "Everyone's still finding their footing here. We just make the best of what we've got."

"Exactly. Another one, Aunty Hai, wishes she had all her tools to show off her skills in making 'bánh chưng' (or sticky rice cakes wrapped in banana leaves, traditionally served during the New Year.) But even something as simple as banana leaves - where would we find them here? And my wife asked me to look for rice paper to make spring rolls. I gave up."

After buying two cans of abalone, the three brothers headed off to pick up two large sheets of poster paper - each nearly half a yard wide - to draw a dragon and write "Happy Year of the Snake" as decorations, bringing a festive Tết atmosphere to the gathering room.

Back at Hiển's house, everyone sat cross-legged around the coffee table, sleeves rolled up, ready to show off their artistic flair. Two boxes of coloring crayons, borrowed from Hiển's son, Tèo, were set out like tools of the trade. Tuất, known for his elegant handwriting, was handed a red board to write the Tết greetings. Meanwhile, Minh and Hiển took charge of drawing a dragon on a white poster, using a reference sketch Hiển had saved from a 'Free Press' article about Tết.

Once finished, the three men stood up and held the two posters side by side, studying them from every angle - back and forth, side to side. Hiển finally frowned and said:

"Why doesn't it feel very Tết-like?"

Minh nodded in agreement.

"If only we had gotten red posters. That would've made it feel more festive."

Tuất suddenly blurted out,

"I know! It's because we're missing a red watermelon."

Minh laughed.

"This guy has a point. So this year, let's feed the Dragon some watermelon."

"Let's do it," Minh said. He raised a red crayon like a brush in an artist's hand, pointed at the dragon, and turned to Hiển.

"Where should we add the watermelon to make it pop?"

Tuất rolled on the floor laughing.

"I've never seen a dragon eat watermelon before!"

Minh slapped his forehead.

"How could I forget? We need firecrackers too! Instead of lion-dance firecrackers, let's have dragon-dance firecrackers!"

And so, the Dragon of 1976 ended up not only feasting on watermelon but also frolicking among piles of bright red firecracker shells. Still, the three brothers weren't quite satisfied with their creation. After draining a can of Coca-Cola, Hiền slapped his thigh and said,

"I've got it!"

He turned to Tuất.

"Your turn. Take the yellow crayon and cover those two boards with apricot blossoms for me."

Tuất eagerly took up the task, leaning over the cardboard with intense focus. Hiền beamed with satisfaction. Minh sat back, studying their handiwork in silence for a moment, then finally nodded.

"Now it really feels like Tết."

After finishing the two panels, Hiền looked at Minh and said,

"Minh, I want to talk to you about something."

"What is it?"

"In the newspaper article about Tết, they called it the Chinese New Year. What do you think about that?"

"I've heard that the Chinese have been in Canada for a long time, since the late 19th century, at least. They came in large groups to work on the railways. Maybe because people here have seen them celebrate Tết for so long, they just got used to calling it that."

"But now that we're here too, they shouldn't keep calling it that."

"Our country is small, tucked away on the other side of the ocean. Most people probably don't even know it exists."

"That's not entirely true. Remember the American press? They used the term 'Tet Offensive' to describe the attacks during the New Year of the Monkey."

"You're right. Now that I think about it, even if people don't know, it's up to us to help them understand."

"Exactly. I'll draft a letter to the editor to explain it properly."

An hour later, after the two brothers had finished drafting the letter by hand, Hiển sat down at the typewriter and began carefully typing a message to the 'Free Press' newspaper, proposing that they refer to 'Tết' as the 'Lunar New Year, a term more inclusive of the many Asian communities who share this celebration, including the Vietnamese.

The first Tết of the Vietnamese diaspora after 1975 arrived in a swirl of excitement and deep nostalgia for home. It came after countless restless days of waiting, though no one quite knew what they were waiting for.

Were they waiting for a soldier's return?

Waiting for a family reunion, to gather around grandparents, arms folded in respect, offering wishes of long life?

Waiting to receive red envelopes?

Waiting for a new set of clothes?

Waiting for the sound of the first firecrackers, to step outside to the ancestral altar, light incense, and offer prayers for the New Year?

Waiting for a friendly card game with a few old friends?

Or simply waiting for those carefree days, riding a bicycle from house to house to visit teachers and classmates?

What dreams still flutter from the wings of spring butterflies?

What remains of those New Year's Eve nights, folding paper money into butterfly shapes to hang on the branches of golden apricot blossoms - nestled behind the polished bronze incense burners, beside a tray of five fruits, next to a watermelon on the altar?

Spring had somehow found its way here, into a small hall beneath a church basement.

Tết had arrived - through a simple gathering with fellow countrymen, through the cherished sounds of the Vietnamese language one had longed so deeply to hear.

The 'Tết' atmosphere here was brought to life with hanging decorations - red and blue balloons, colorful paper streamers draped across the ceiling - all thoughtfully arranged under the direction of Father Swanson, who had invited everyone to help decorate the room in celebration of the Lunar New Year with the community.

In addition, two themed panels created by Hưởng were mounted on a green board placed at the far end of the room.

With warm enthusiasm, Father Swanson led the gathering in singing "Kumbaya" to honor God. In truth, it was more of a gentle humming, "Kum-ba-ya... Kum-ba-ya..."

Afterward, Father Swanson happily took on the role of a village elder, handing out lucky money envelopes to the children. Given his age, he was more than qualified to be their grandfather. Red envelopes were also prepared for the children of the local volunteers who had helped organize this first-ever 'Tết' celebration for the community.

Once the festivities had come to a close, Uncle Quý, one of the respected elders in the community, volunteered to lead the traditional 'Tết' couplet game. He delighted everyone with his elegant, meaningful verses, spirited delivery, and charismatic charm. The couplet he proudly presented, which he claimed had remained unmatched for decades, was one attributed to Thế Lữ, the renowned poet and writer of the 1930s.

Tuất, being young and never one to back down from a challenge, eagerly raised his hand to respond with a couplet of his own, composed on the spot. His reply may not have been destined for literary immortality, but it had one undeniable effect: it sent the entire room into fits of laughter.

The hall echoed with joy. For a brief moment, all worries melted away. One by one, people began to leave - some wrapped in heavy coats, others bundled in parkas, some in tall boots, a few in rain boots - each confidently stepping out into the biting night air. Outside, it was minus twenty degrees Celsius, and yet they trekked ten, fifteen, even twenty minutes through the snow to reach home.

The new year had begun - and it had to begin. For oneself, for one's children, for loved ones still in the homeland - each carrying their own hopes, burdens, and quiet dreams.

13. The Miner

Tuất had to work an extra half-hour of overtime, leaving the garage late. His stomach was growling with hunger. He hurried to the Submarine Sandwich restaurant on Portage Avenue, which cuts across the main downtown shopping district, hoping to satisfy his craving. Sitting down, he munched on a long loaf of bread that filled both hands, eating quickly so he'd have time to wash up before the 20-minute walk to night school.

As the Vietnamese saying goes, "Near ink, you get stained; near light, you shine." Sharing a dwelling with young navy officers who all had plans to return to school and continue their education, Tuất found inspiration. He, too, had a plan. He started with night English classes and was now attending an adult high school, aiming to earn his diploma, the first step toward enrolling in a trade school to study car mechanics.

The eatery was nearly empty at this hour, with just a few vacant tables scattered around. Suddenly, a young Asian-looking person approached Tuất's table and asked in English, "Are you Vietnamese?"

Tuất looked up, surprised.

"How did you know?"

"I saw the news. Over seventy Vietnamese refugees have arrived here in the past few months."

"But still, how could you tell I'm one of them?"

"I come here often, and until recently, I rarely saw anyone who looked Asian."

Tuất, now curious, asked, "Where are you from?"

"Malaysia. I'm a student at the University of Manitoba."

Tuất was happy to have someone to talk to, but he had to excuse himself - he needed to finish his sandwich and make it to class on time. As he picked up his food again, the Malaysian friend asked with interest, "So, you're going to night school?"

Tuất nodded while chewing on his bread. The Malaysian student gave him a sympathetic look.

"It must be difficult, having to work and study at the same time."

Tuất didn't expect a stranger to understand his situation so well. He put the sandwich down, glanced outside, and said quietly, "It's really tough. I don't know if I can keep going like this for two more years just to finish high school."

The Malaysian student nodded in understanding.

"At one point, I tried doing both, working and studying, but I felt completely drained. I didn't have the patience or energy to keep it up."

"So what did you do?" Tuất asked.

"I decided to work hard for a short while at a high-paying job. Then I saved enough money to enroll in full-time studies. That way, I could focus better on school and assignments."

Tuất's eyes widened with interest.

"What kind of work did you do?"

"There were two jobs I tried. At first, a friend introduced me to working as a train attendant on the cross-country trains in Canada, selling food or serving in the first-class cars. Just a few months of summer work was enough to pay for a whole year of schooling."

Tuất exclaimed with excitement, "That sounds great!"

But the Malaysian student shook his head.

"It was actually very tiring. Each trip from Vancouver to Montreal— or the other way around - took more than four days straight. You had to eat and sleep on the train, surrounded by noise and constant motion. It was hard to get any real rest. After that summer, I switched to working in the North, for a mining company."

"Coal mines?" Tuất asked.

"No, I worked at a nickel mine. Getting there wasn't easy - it takes two flights from here. It's really remote, no airports nearby. First, you fly almost two hours north to the city of Thompson. Then you transfer to a small plane that lands in an open clearing near the mine, actually, closer to the workers' dormitories."

Hearing this, Tuất began to feel a bit hesitant. 'If it's already this cold here,' he thought, 'then how much colder must it be in the far north of Canada?' The Malaysian friend seemed to pick up on his concern and added reassuringly:

"Sure, it's freezing outside up there, but the camps have heating stoves inside. I worked for four months and saved enough to cover nearly two years of school."

Tuất's enthusiasm returned. He leaned forward, eager to learn more. "How do you apply for a job like that?"

The Malaysian student pulled a pen from his pocket, scribbled the company's address onto a paper napkin, and slid it across the table to Tuất.

That night, after returning from school, Tuất lay alone on his bed, staring at the ceiling. He thought long and hard, deep into the night, about a kind of job he had never considered before - one no one he knew had ever mentioned: working as a miner.

Tuất tried to imagine what mining might be like. In his mind's eye, he pictured a dry pit where several men dug steadily, inch by inch, into the earth. Around them, women in conical hats moved back and forth, carrying baskets of soil. The digging continued from morning until night, day after day. The pit grew deeper and deeper until, eventually, the miners reached the metal they were after. Tuất wasn't sure what kind of metal it was - his Malaysian friend had mentioned it, but the name hadn't stuck.

Once again, he tried to envision whether he could endure such a job. He pictured himself bundled in Eskimo-style clothing, head and ears covered, standing in the biting cold, digging all day while his hands and feet grew numb.

Tuất moved through these thoughts as though walking in a haze - his mind tangled between dream and reality, between the construction sites he had once watched with fascination in Vietnam after first arriving in Saigon, and the frozen landscapes of Canada.

Upon waking, Tuất suddenly recalled a folk saying his father used to repeat:

"No one in this world escapes hardship. Hardship exists, but so does the moment of being rewarded with leisure."

With renewed determination, Tuất quickly finished his breakfast and headed to the auto repair shop. He planned to ask for permission to apply for the mining job during his lunch break.

After lunch, Tuất made his way to the address his Malaysian friend had given him. It was in a small town - a modest hub with a few streets branching out to various company offices. He found the right place easily enough, but the language barrier proved challenging. Fortunately, he met a kind and patient secretary who was willing to help. The application process involved a stack of forms and required several signatures, but Tuất followed her instructions as best he could, relying on her guidance.

She handed him a pen and pointed to each spot where he needed to sign. And just like that, it was done. Tuất was now a miner.

'That wasn't so hard,' he thought.

The secretary told him to return the following week to pick up his flight ticket.

Three weeks later, Tuất arrived at the nickel mining area north of Thompson, a city in Manitoba province. The Cessna 206, a small five-seat airplane, touched down on a makeshift landing strip about 200 meters from the four cabins that made up the miners' camp. Two one-ton pickup trucks were waiting to pick up Tuất and two other miners from the same flight, along with various supplies and luggage headed to the camp.

He arrived at the camp at 11:30 AM. After following the driver to the sleeping quarters to drop off his belongings, Tuất made his way to the management office, where he was greeted by a middle-aged man with a sturdy build and a face almost entirely hidden by a reddish beard.

"I'm Mike," the man introduced himself.

"I'm Tuất," he replied.

Mike squinted, asking him to repeat it. After the third try, he offered with a chuckle, "I'll call you Toot, OK?"

Tuất smiled and nodded in agreement.

Mike handed him an apron. "You can head to the front and grab some lunch. Normally, it's better to eat a bit earlier - some of the crews start coming in around 11:30."

While Tuất was still trying to make sense of Mike's words, he was led to the dining hall and introduced to Tom - a young man with a fair complexion, an apron tied around his waist, and a ready smile. Mike asked Tom to show Tuất the ropes, then waved goodbye and left.

Tom shook Tuất's hand.

"You go eat first. After that, there's plenty of work to do."

Tuất asked, "What will I be doing?"

"I'll explain later," Tom replied. "But basically, once the workers finish their meals, you'll clear the tables. Then head inside to wash the dishes."

Tuất looked confused. "When do I go to the mine?"

Tom blinked. "Why would you go there?"

"Isn't that where we're supposed to work?"

Tom laughed, a bit baffled. "No, I've never even set foot in the mine."

Tuất was stunned. He had signed up to be a miner - so why wasn't he being sent to the mine?

Over the next few days, through a mix of gestures and broken English, he managed to piece together the truth from his coworkers. It turned out he was working for a catering company contracted to provide three meals a day for the miners. His actual job was to help maintain the dining area and wash dishes - not dig for nickel.

All those sleepless nights had been for nothing. If this was all the job required, Tuất thought, it was actually quite enjoyable. It truly did seem like the land of opportunity, just as his fellow compatriots at Pendleton camp had often said. The pay was relatively high, and the company covered all expenses - meals, lodging, and transportation. At this rate, Tuất calculated, after just four months of work, he'd be sitting on a small fortune.

To him, true wealth meant more than just money - it meant easing some of the financial burden so he could focus on his studies.

When he returned to Winnipeg four months later, what surprised his friends and fellow countrymen even more than his financial success was his newfound fluency in English. Not only was Tuất rich in savings, he was now rich in vocabulary. Jokingly, people started calling him the "Son of Canada," because his speech was now peppered with English phrases like "Sorry" and "Thank you."

And when he got excited, Tuất often blurted out exclamations that left the locals doing a double take - things like "Wow! Oh my God! Really!" or, more endearingly, "Oh my goodness!"

In the beginning, fellow Vietnamese sought one another out just for the chance to speak their native tongue. How could anyone possibly master English as quickly as Tuất had? For four months, due to his circumstances, Tuất had no choice but to speak and listen to English all day long - sometimes even in his dreams. Upon waking, he would often chuckle, imagining his grandmother proudly telling the neighbors, "My grandson even talks in English while he's sleeping!"

The money Tuất saved from the job, originally intended for mining work, enabled him to enroll in full-time education. From then on, he only needed to work summer jobs at local shops. With his full attention on his studies, it didn't take long for him to earn his high school diploma, gain admission to a community college, and eventually graduate with a degree in heating and air conditioning systems (HAVC).

He had chosen this field based on a friend's advice: compared to automotive repair, HVAC work was lighter, cleaner, and more in demand. Every apartment, every house, every building needed some kind of climate control system - something always in need of maintenance or repair. It was a job that promised stability. Tuất would never have to worry about being out of work.

14. The Road To 'Glory'

Tuất's sheer hard work and dedication to his studies had finally paid off. The boy who once apprenticed at Uncle Bảy's garage - so talented that he left Mr. Sáu "Navigator" thoroughly impressed - had now graduated from... MIT. At least, that's how his soldier brothers liked to say it, brimming with admiration, as though Tuất had earned a degree from the world-renowned Massachusetts Institute of Technology. In reality, he had attended the Manitoba Institute of Technology.

But for students, graduating is only one part of the journey; the next challenge is finding a job. Success in university depends heavily on one's abilities and diligence, but job placement is another matter altogether - shaped by the economy, social conditions, and sometimes even politics. Some people attribute their employment status to fate. There are those who receive job offers before they even graduate, and others who, years after finishing school, still struggle to find work in their chosen field.

Tuất's case was an exception - one not easily summed up in a word or two.

Throughout his years of study, Tuất spent every summer working at the same auto repair shop he had connected with shortly after arriving in Canada. By the time he graduated, both the manager and the chief mechanic had come to know his skills well - and were genuinely impressed. He had truly lived up to his reputation as the disciple of Uncle Bảy "de Song."

Tuất was warmly offered a full-time position with a salary equivalent to that of a mechanic with ten years of experience, according to the manager, even though Tuất had only accumulated about three years of hands-on experience, and that mostly during summer breaks.

He didn't hesitate for a moment in making his decision. Rather than continue searching for a job in the field he had formally studied, he joyfully accepted the generous offer. His heart had never strayed far from Uncle Bảy's garage, and now it led him right back to the world of auto repair. Besides, he reasoned, the knowledge he had gained about heating and air conditioning systems in school wouldn't go to waste - it could still be applied to the climate control systems in vehicles, or even to engine cooling mechanisms.

Unbeknownst to him, his career choice had set him on the "road to glory," as some soldier friends would tease - though they were quick to add, "or the path to mishap."

After working for more than two months, one Friday afternoon, Tuất noticed a young man bringing in a Mustang for repairs. The manager declined the job, explaining that the shop was too busy - four cars still needed to be completed in time for customer pickup. The young man, however, pleaded persistently, eventually revealing, "I really need the car by Saturday. It's my sister's wedding, and I have to join the convoy."

Tuất overheard the conversation and felt sorry for him.

Later that day, after clocking out and walking to the parking lot, Tuất unexpectedly saw the young man still waiting, clearly holding out hope that a mechanic might free up at the last minute. Curious, Tuất approached him.

"Still here?" Tuất asked.

The young man nodded and explained, "The suspension failed around noon. Now, every time I hit a bump, there's a loud clanging sound underneath - like something's loose or hitting the frame."

Tuất offered, "Let's take it for a quick drive. I'll see what I can figure out."

A few minutes into the ride, Tuất smiled and said, "I think I know what's going on."

Worried, the young man, whose name was Roy, asked, "Is it serious?"

"I don't think so," Tuất replied. "Can you pull over somewhere? I'd like to take a closer look."

They turned onto a quiet side road and brought the car to a stop. Tuất stepped out, walked to the rear of the vehicle, and began pressing down on each side with his hands. The Mustang rocked from side to side, and with each motion came the unmistakable clanging noise from underneath.

Roy exclaimed excitedly, "That's it! That's the exact sound I've been hearing while driving!"

Tuất bent down, peering into a narrow corner behind the rear wheel. After examining the suspension, he pointed and said, "It's that part - the suspension bracket. It's damaged."

Roy leaned in. "Can you fix it?"

"I don't have the tools with me," Tuất replied. "But you can still drive it - it's not dangerous."

Roy shook his head. "Still, showing up to my sister's wedding with the car rattling like this wouldn't be great."

After a brief pause, he offered, "What if I take you to a place I know? We've got all the tools there. You could use them to help me fix it."

Tuất didn't hesitate. "Alright - but first, you'll need to buy a new suspension bracket. Hopefully the parts shop is still open. If you can get one, I'll install it for you."

After purchasing the necessary parts, Roy took Tuất to what looked like an abandoned garage. Grass pushed up through the cracks in the parking lot, and tall weeds lined the sidewalk along the walls. But Roy had a key to the front door and confidently led Tuất inside.

The moment they stepped into the workshop, Tuất looked around in awe. It felt as though he had stepped back into Uncle Bảy's old garage. Everything was so familiar - the vise clamped firmly to one corner of the workbench, the rows of wrenches hanging neatly on the wall, and the scattered screwdriver sets resting beside two olive-green toolboxes, clearly repurposed military ammunition crates.

It was nothing like the modern shop where Tuất now worked, but the space radiated the same spirit, the same sense of purpose. The resemblance to Uncle Bảy's garage was uncanny.

Tuất was momentarily stunned - unexpectedly transported back to a familiar scene from his homeland, thousands of miles away. Without trouble, he located the tools he needed, and just half an hour later, Roy was behind the wheel, taking a test drive around the city with a wide grin on his face.

"It's even quieter than before!" Roy exclaimed. "Thank you so, so much!"

Eventually, he turned to Tuất and asked, "So, how much do I owe you?"

Realizing Roy genuinely wanted to pay, Tuất shook his head and said, "You don't owe me anything."

Roy insisted, but Tuất stood firm in his refusal.

"Then at least let me treat you to dinner," Roy offered. "Where do you like to eat?"

Seeing how sincere Roy was, Tuất replied with a smile, "I usually go to the Submarine sandwich place."

Roy laughed heartily. "You're easygoing, huh? Don't you like fancy restaurants? Just kidding - wherever you like, that's where we're going."

Later, sitting across from Roy at the fast-food joint, Tuất had a chance to observe him more closely. Despite his rugged, sun-darkened appearance, Roy carried an easygoing charm. His wide, bright smile seemed to light up his whole face before he even spoke. Yet his eyes were constantly alert, darting around as if he were expecting someone - or maybe just out of habit, always scanning his surroundings.

After finishing their meal, the two exchanged phone numbers before saying goodbye. Roy gripped Tuất's hand firmly and said, "From now on, we're friends. If you ever need anything, call me. I'll do whatever I can to help."

After an eventful weekend, Tuất returned to the workshop as usual. Around noon, the manager called him into the office. Someone had reported seeing Tuất leave the parking lot with a potential customer the previous Friday, and the manager wanted an explanation.

Tuất calmly recounted the entire incident - how he had helped Roy out of kindness, after work hours, without using any of the company's resources.

But the manager's face grew stern. Then, in a cold, flat voice, he said, "You've violated company policy. You can't work here anymore. Go to the secretary's office, collect your final paycheck."

Tuất stood there, stunned. He didn't understand what rule he had broken. But one glance at the manager's hard, almost hostile expression filled him with fear. He lowered his head and obeyed silently, not daring to ask any questions.

Perhaps it was a habit rooted in his upbringing - never questioning authority, for fear it would be seen as insolent or disrespectful. Better to remain in the dark, he had always believed, than to risk offending those in charge.

He walked home in a daze, his steps heavy with confusion and sorrow. As he neared the house, it suddenly struck him: 'The manager must have thought I was stealing customers - doing private jobs on the side.'

The more he thought about it, the more convinced he became. It was a painful misunderstanding, but one that now seemed irreversible.

Tuất had intended to return to the factory the next morning to offer the manager a full explanation, hoping to clear up any misunderstanding. Yet each time he recalled the manager's cold demeanor that afternoon, Tuất hesitated, weighed down by a growing sense of dismay. He couldn't understand how the manager's attitude had shifted so abruptly. Just that morning, the man had been his usual cheerful self, chatting with a smile. But in the blink of an eye, his face had hardened, and he dismissed Tuất as though harboring a long-standing grudge. The sudden turn left Tuất feeling deeply wounded and unjustly accused. The sting of being misunderstood, coupled with the manager's harshness, lingered painfully in his heart. That evening, unable to shake the heaviness, he skipped cooking dinner altogether.

Instead, he wandered down the street in search of something to eat. The Submarine Sandwich shop was the closest, but just as he approached, a sobering thought struck him: he was now unemployed. 'Would I be able to find another job soon?' he wondered. Up to now,

Tuất had lived frugally and managed to save a modest amount in the bank - what might seem small to others, but to him, was a hard-earned fortune. Still, he reminded himself, 'In times like these, with the future so uncertain, I must learn to live within my means.'

Tuất quickly changed direction, muttering a familiar saying among his compatriots: "If you want to avoid going into debt, go to McDonald's." At this fast food chain, he usually ordered a thin hamburger and a small cup of Coke - just enough to fill his stomach, and all for barely a dollar. But tonight, facing the weight of the day's misfortune, he tightened his belt even further. He skipped the Coke and asked for a cup of cold water instead.

He tried to shake off the bitter incident from that afternoon, but the manager's cold, resentful expression refused to leave his thoughts. As he sat at the table, his half-eaten hamburger pushed aside, Tuất stared out the window, searching for an explanation. Suddenly, the image of Mr. Sáu, nicknamed "Navigator", rose in his memory. A mentor and fatherly figure, Mr. Sáu had once told him, "Westerners tend to act more from reason than emotion, while our people often do the opposite." He had gone on to say, "Although we have a saying that 'anger clouds the mind,' we don't always live by it."

But what struck Tuất most was how Mr. Sáu had warned, "Reason, when used to silence conscience, becomes dangerous. That's how Western powers once justified slavery and colonization - arguing their way through logic while ignoring human suffering."

When Tuất compared Mr. Sáu's words to his own experiences with Westerners, he couldn't help but feel puzzled. Since the day he arrived in Canada, every local person he had encountered had shown sincere sympathy toward him and his fellow countrymen - refugees who had landed here by chance. Their kindness wasn't just in words; it manifested in tangible, wholehearted actions. They offered support, lent guidance, and eased the newcomers through the most difficult early days of resettlement. Each time Tuất reflected on this, his heart swelled with a desire to someday repay their generosity. In letters to his parents back home, he often described the warmth and compassion of the Canadian people. So he didn't believe that Westerners were emotionless or ruled purely by logic. If anything, their empathy left him all the more confused about his manager's sudden, cold behavior.

As Tuất reached the door of his rented room, he heard the phone ringing inside. He rushed in and picked it up.

"Toot? Roy here. I've been calling you all afternoon."

When they first met earlier, Tuất had agreed to go by that 'English name' for Roy's convenience.

"I went out to eat," Tuất replied.

"Did you eat at the Submarine Sandwich place?"

"No, I had McDonald's."

"Oh, that doesn't count as dinner. Wait for me - I'm coming to take you out for a proper meal. Okay?"

After several failed attempts to politely decline, Tuất finally agreed. Roy drove him to a restaurant on the outskirts of town. From the outside, it looked like an old wooden house, but it had a certain grandeur thanks to its oversized lot - large enough to accommodate two spacious parking areas for guests.

Roy pulled into the side lot and parked.

"We're waiting for my boss," he said, turning to Tuất. "Just call him Mister C. for short."

Early in the day, after hearing Roy recount their weekend encounter, Mister C. had expressed keen interest and insisted on meeting Tuất in person.

Not long after Roy and Tuất began waiting, a sleek black Cadillac pulled into the lot and stopped beside Roy's car. Roy quickly stepped forward to open the door. A man wearing a wide-brimmed black hat that shaded most of his forehead stepped out. After Roy's brief introduction, the man looked at Tuất and offered a gentle smile. That was Mr. C.

Roy and Tuất followed him toward the restaurant. To Tuất's surprise, Mr. C. led them to a side entrance rather than through the main front door like the other patrons. They stepped into a dimly lit interior that felt completely separate from the busy atmosphere outside.

As soon as Tuất crossed the threshold, his eyes widened in amazement. It felt as though he had wandered into a royal palace, like one he had seen in the movie 'Napoleon the Great.' Above him, a massive chandelier shimmered with thousands of tiny lights, casting a golden glow through cascading strands of crystal. Beneath it stood an enormous round table made of black ebony, surrounded by eight imposing chairs upholstered in thick green leather. Bathed in warm light, the entire setting radiated grandeur and solemnity, arranged as though to welcome someone of great importance.

Tuất suddenly realized that this was a private dining room, separated from the main dining area at the front of the restaurant by a solid wall. Mr. C. pulled out a chair and seated himself beneath a large portrait of an elderly woman, nearly a meter tall, surrounded by smaller black-and-white photographs - presumably family members from different generations.

Before ordering food, Mr. C. asked Tuất what kind of wine he preferred. Tuất hesitated, unsure how to respond - he had never drunk wine before. Then, a vague memory surfaced from his time in

Vietnam: someone once said, "Red wine nourishes the blood." Blinking, he replied, "Red wine."

After taking his first sip, Tuất eagerly answered Mr. C.'s questions about his vocational training journey, from Vietnam to Canada. With the second sip, then the third, his head began to spin. He couldn't recall what he said after that, but one moment remained vivid in his memory: the shock he felt when Mr. C. made an unexpected proposal.

"Do I really own the garage?" Tuất wondered, unsure if he had misheard or misunderstood Mr. C. The garage where he had gone to borrow tools to fix Roy's car the previous weekend was indeed owned by Mr. C. - and now he wanted Tuất to "take care of it."

As Mr. C. explained, he had once leased the garage to a cousin who was both a skilled mechanic and the manager. Unfortunately, about six months ago, the cousin had died suddenly of a heart attack. Since then, Mr. C. hadn't been able to find a trustworthy replacement. Now, impressed by Tuất's skill and generosity in helping Roy, he wanted to offer Tuất the opportunity to manage the garage.

Tuất felt as though he had stepped into the story of 'The Rich Man Who Lost His Horse.' What had seemed like a misfortune - meeting Roy and getting fired - had turned into unexpected luck. He never imagined that from knowing Roy, he would end up "rising straight into the clouds and becoming the Uncle Bảy 'de Song' of Canada."

This morning, the sky was clear and blue, and warm sunlight poured into the garage. Tuất smiled as he looked at the pot of roses - still proudly displayed in the accounting office - sent to celebrate the garage's opening day. Mr. C. had entrusted Tuất with full control over the repair work, along with three young apprentices learning the trade. As for the finances, daily expenses and revenues, Tuất didn't have to worry. Mr. C. had arranged for a professional accountant to set up an office right in the garage to handle all of it.

After a few months of learning the ropes as a garage "owner," Tuất
had gradually come to embody the seasoned qualities of Uncle Bảy
'de Song.' He was now measured in every step, thoughtful in every
word, and had even begun applying the trade secrets that had made
Uncle Bảy legendary. Whenever a car, new or old, was brought in,
Tuất would gently advise its cash-strapped owner to be ready to
replace the steering bar on their next visit.

The garage has grown increasingly busy, and by all signs, business
must be thriving. Tuất doesn't know the exact figures - those are
handled entirely by the accountant - but he feels fortunate and
completely satisfied with his current salary, which is three times
higher than what he earned in his previous job. And that's not even
counting the extra pay he receives when Mr. C.'s associates
occasionally send him to repair heaters or air conditioners at nearby
shops.

Of course, in life, money isn't everything. How people treat one
another matters just as much, if not more. In this regard, Tuất also
considers himself lucky, no less than any of his fellow countrymen.
Most of them deeply appreciate the genuine, almost affectionate
kindness they've experienced from the local community, from the
factory floors to the small businesses. It stands in stark contrast to the
rumors and warnings they once heard in the refugee camps about
racism or cultural conflicts in the new land.

Tuất considered himself fortunate never to have encountered any
unpleasantness in his interactions with those around him. On the
contrary, he often felt respected - and perhaps even admired a bit
more than was warranted - by both his colleagues and many of his
clients. At first, he had been unsure how to relate to the young
apprentice mechanics and the frequent visitors who roared into the
garage on motorcycles. They sometimes came for repairs, sometimes
just to chat. With their arms covered in unusual tattoos - some inked
all the way up to their necks - and their swaggering demeanor, they

gave off the impression of belonging to a tight-knit, somewhat mysterious group. They appeared rebellious, even defiant. Yet, to Tuất's surprise, they treated him with utmost courtesy. Every conversation with him was peppered with respectful "Yes, sir" and "No, sir."

Three years later, on a warm, sunny spring morning, the tulip garden beside the garage burst into vivid red bloom. Tuất stood at the center of the shop, calmly directing his team with a wave of his hand, each gesture like a conductor leading an orchestra. In his other hand, he cradled a cup of fine Jamaican coffee, savoring every milligram of its rich flavor - an indulgent taste of the success he had built for himself.

Then, without warning, the sharp blare of sirens shattered the moment. Red lights flashed furiously across the hoods of several police cruisers that had pulled up outside. Alarms wailed. Chaos erupted.

Three of the mechanics bolted out the back door in a panic, looking for a way to flee. Right behind them, the accountant followed suit, clutching his bag tightly as he ran.

Tuất remained frozen, still trying to make sense of what was happening, when a chorus of shouts rang out from every direction:

"Hands up! Hands up!"

Tuất was apprehended and placed in a waiting police van parked by the roadside. The three mechanics and the accountant were also arrested shortly after fleeing through the back door of the garage. At the police station, Tuất was fortunately released after just two hours of questioning. A few days later, media reports began to reveal details that shed light on the shocking turn of events.

As it turned out, the previous owner of the garage, unrelated to Mr. C., had struggled with a severe gambling addiction. To feed his habit, he mortgaged the garage, eventually losing it to Mr. C., a well-known figure in the local criminal underworld. After acquiring the property, Mr. C. used the garage as a front to launder money and obscure illicit profits from other criminal operations.

Over the two years of investigation leading up to the takedown of Mr. C.'s money laundering operation, the police had developed a clear understanding of Tuất's role. They recognized that he had no involvement in the criminal activities and chose not to press any charges against him - though they did issue a few stern warnings.

In the days that followed, during drinking sessions with his former military "brothers," Tuất's unexpected ordeal became a favorite topic of conversation - always met with amused remarks and teasing banter. Though they were speaking about Tuất, it often felt as if they were reflecting on themselves as well:

"For most people, once they graduate, the road to glory stretches wide ahead. But for you, it's one misadventure after another."

In truth, the "you" in their stories could easily apply to any student from Saigon whose education was interrupted by conscription. A high school graduate would be drafted before having a chance to attend college. A university graduate would see their dream career stall at the starting line.

Tuất, a young man from Vietnam, was not someone who surrendered easily to fate. His motto had always been: "If at first you don't succeed, try again." Though he might have suffered from the syndrome of "stepping on a watermelon rind and then fearing coconut shells," by the very next morning, he was already out searching for a new job.

He wandered the city, knocking on the doors of shops where he had previously done repair or installation work on their heating or cooling systems. This time, he introduced himself not as a mechanic doing odd jobs, but as a "Professional Heating and Air Conditioning Technician."

A Vietnamese-Canadian accountant in town helped Tuất formally establish a repair business. Tuất became both the owner and the director. When the registration papers came through, he was startled to see the official title: "President Tuat Van Nguyen."

Tuất chuckled - he hadn't expected a title that sounded more like the leader of a country than the head of a small HVAC company.

Over time, Tuất began to understand the true nature of his relationships with some of his former clients. After starting his own company, he lost quite a few shop owners who had originally come to him under the influence, or pressure, of Mr. C. Tuất didn't mind. He believed it was better to steer clear of the so-called Godfather's shadow, even if that shadow no longer lingered.

The clients who remained loyal were mostly Vietnamese-owned nail salons. Among them was Sister Five, who had been trying for weeks to convince Tuất to buy her business. Back in Vietnam, her husband, Brother Five, had been a barber, while she painted nails for women in the neighborhood. After immigrating to Canada, the couple spent a few months learning the trade and eventually opened a small shop that combined both services: barbering and nail care.

Sadly, just a few months earlier, Brother Five had fallen gravely ill and passed away, leaving Sister Five to manage everything on her own.

Around noon, Tuất stopped by Sister Five's shop to let her know he'd be away on vacation for a week. After three years of being "President," business had finally settled into a steady rhythm, and Tuất was eager to take his newly purchased Ford Mustang out for a long-awaited road trip.

Sister Five asked with a teasing smile,

"Where are you planning to go? Little Saigon? I heard there are tons of Vietnamese over there - and so much fun. You can find any dish you're craving."

Little Saigon, often called the capital of the Vietnamese diaspora, had recently been officially established near Los Angeles, California. It had quickly become a magnet for Vietnamese refugees from across North America, all drawn by the hope of finding a taste of home on foreign soil.

Tuất was no exception - he was excited to see it with his own eyes.

"Yes, I've heard stories from our friends who went there and got really excited," Tuất said.

Before he could leave, Sister Five suddenly made a proposal.

"Or… how about you buy this salon? I'll offer you a good deal."

Tuất was caught off guard - he hadn't even considered the idea.

"But I don't know how to cut hair or do nails," he replied.

"That's okay," Sister Five said warmly. "I've known you for years, and I can see you're a very capable person. You can do anything."

Before she could finish the sentence, Tuất glanced around the shop and shook his head.

"Thank you, Sister, but if I took over this place, I'd probably just stand around and watch - not knowing what to do."

"Don't worry," she reassured him. "I'll stay on to help. You're such a handyman - you could convert the barbershop section into another nail station. All you'd need is one more pedicure chair and to hire a nail technician to work with us."

Tuất found Sister Five's suggestions somewhat convincing, but his mind was already set on exploring California, especially Little Saigon. Once again, he politely found a way to excuse himself.

"Alright, I'll think about it and let you know when I'm back in a few days."

"Okay, stay safe," she replied.

As Tuất reached the door, Sister Five called out after him.

"Oh, and make sure you don't come back empty-handed!"

Tuất assumed she was hinting at bringing back some Vietnamese food to share with friends, so he quickly replied,

"Don't worry - just save your appetite for the fruits I'll bring back."

Sister Five burst out laughing.

"I wasn't asking you to buy anything! I meant: leave single, return double. Try to find yourself a girlfriend and get married!"

Tuất chuckled shyly and waved goodbye.

15. Golden Palanquin

After bidding farewell to Sister Five and the other clients, Tuất set off alone, driving his brand-new Ford Mustang on a journey of over three thousand kilometers toward Los Angeles. He had two possible routes in mind - one that would take him through the United States starting from Minnesota, just south of his home province of Manitoba, and another that would carry him across western Canada. In the end, he chose the latter, charting a course through Manitoba, Saskatchewan, Alberta, and British Columbia, before turning south along the Pacific coast through two American states to reach the heart of the Vietnamese refugee community near Los Angeles.

Tuất was eager to explore the vast country that had offered him refuge, spurred by glowing stories from friends who had made the trip before him. After his first day on the road, his car rolled steadily across the endless prairie, a sea of fertile farmland and rocky wilderness stretching to the horizon. Gradually, the majestic outline of mountains emerged in the distance. Eventually, he arrived in Banff, the destination he had long looked forward to - an alpine resort town perched high on the slopes of the Rocky Mountains. There, the natural landscape unfolded like a painting, with mountains mirrored in crystal-clear lakes, and every view more breathtaking than the last.

Under the clear blue sky, towering rows of pine trees lined the hillside, descending gently toward the emerald-colored lakes below, as if slipping into a dreamlike realm. Along the famous shores of Lake Louise, clusters of Japanese tourists moved about, shifting from one side to the other, their camera lenses scanning the landscape in search of the perfect angle. Yet, no matter how many shots they took, none seemed to satisfy them. The lake remained serene and silent, lost in its own stillness, while people wandered curiously along its edge, chasing an elusive sense of perfection.

As Tuất took in the view, his eyes were drawn to a Japanese girl who stood apart from the crowd. Unlike the others, she wasn't taking pictures. She stood motionless beside a pine tree, quietly gazing at the lake, now and then lifting her eyes to the jagged mountain peaks carved into the sky or to a drifting cluster of white clouds. Something in her demeanor stirred a memory - of Hoa, who often seemed lost in her own private world. Despite the increasing number of letters arriving from home, none had ever come from her.

Tuất wondered what Hoa might be doing at that very moment. Beyond the endless mountain range before him lay the road to the sea, and across the distant Pacific stood a moss-green house. Behind its low fence, beneath the shade of an old jackfruit tree, rested a stone grinder against the weathered wooden frame. Perhaps Hoa was there now, crouched beside it, grinding flour to help her mother make sticky rice cakes for the morning market.

Just then, the Japanese girl shifted and quietly followed her tour group to another spot. Tuất blinked, momentarily disoriented, and instinctively murmured a folk verse, as if offering a soft reproach to the landscape itself:

'*Núi cao chi lắm núi ơi,*
Núi che mặt trời chẳng thấy người thương.'

(Oh mountains, mountains, towering high,
You block the sun - my love, I cannot find.)

The following day, Tuất drove over the mountain pass and descended into Vancouver - a bustling, prosperous city on Canada's west coast. Early the next morning, he made his way downtown, eager to find a restaurant recommended by fellow countrymen, renowned for serving authentic 'phở', the iconic Vietnamese noodle soup from the northern region of the country.

As he cruised down a quiet street, his eyes scanned the shop signs lining the road. Then, "Ah, here it is!" Tuất exclaimed, heart lifting at the sight of the words 'Phở Sài Gòn'. His excitement wasn't merely that of a hungry man finding a place to eat. It was deeper than that, the thrill of a homesick soul catching a fleeting glimpse of home. The sign bore every familiar accent and diacritic - each curve and mark a reminder of his native tongue, from the round, egg-like "O" to the bearded "Ơ," and the delicate tonal strokes that shaped meaning and melody. In that moment, Tuất felt as though he had stumbled upon something precious he thought he had lost - a small, sacred fragment of his homeland, shining through the glass of a shopfront in a foreign land.

Back in Banff, Tuất had noticed how many public signs and tourist directions were written in Japanese, and a quiet wish had taken root in his heart - that one day, he might see Vietnamese given the same recognition. Today, perhaps buoyed by a particularly cheerful mood, he smiled with quiet satisfaction when he spotted, amid a forest of shop signs, the three words 'Phở Sài Gòn' proudly displayed under the North American sky.

Inside, the restaurant was spacious and tastefully decorated in a distinctly Vietnamese style. Two rustic paintings adorned the walls, alongside three lacquer panels that celebrated the beauty of the homeland through images of women dressed in traditional attire from northern, central, and southern Vietnam. Tuất felt a sense of wonder, as though he were rediscovering the essence of his country in this distant corner of the world. But what touched him even more were the sounds - the familiar cadence of Vietnamese laughter, animated conversation, and background music. Though as lively as a bustling market, it was precisely the kind of joyful noise he hadn't realized he was missing. After years of quiet longing, it filled a void he had silently carried with him.

The restaurant was bustling, with only two empty tables left. A young Vietnamese man approached and, speaking in Vietnamese, said, "Please take table number six." Somehow, being greeted in his native language - by a fellow Vietnamese, in a Vietnamese restaurant - felt both oddly unfamiliar and deeply comforting to Tuất. He couldn't help but marvel at how something so ordinary could stir such warmth.

He had barely settled into his seat when a voice called out from the next table, "Brother Tuất!" Startled, Tuất turned and saw Trọng - Mr. Hai Sang's son - whom he had once briefly tutored. Trọng beamed with excitement. It took Tuất a second to place the familiar face, but then recognition dawned. His eyes widened in surprise, and a rush of joy swept through him - an indescribable feeling that lit up his expression.

But as Mr. Hai Sang, seated beside his son, turned to look, the smile on Tuất's lips faltered. He lowered his gaze and offered a polite, almost sheepish greeting: "Hello, Mr. Hai."

After a quiet prompt from his son reminding him of their guest's identity, Mr. Hai Sang softened and waved Tuất over. He invited him to join their table and began chatting warmly, as if nothing awkward had ever passed between them. Much to Tuất's relief, Mr. Hai Sang - whether out of kindness or forgetfulness - made no mention of the day Tuất had come to his house in Saigon to retrieve the toolbox before leaving not just the city, but the country itself.

Through his conversation with Mr. Hai Sang, Tuất learned that back in Vietnam, he had owned a shrimp fishing boat used for export. On the final, chaotic day of the war, it was that very boat that carried him and his family out of the country, eventually reaching the Philippines. What struck Tuất even more was learning that Mr. Tư, Mr. Hai Sang's driver, had accompanied his family on that voyage. According to Mr.

Hai Sang, Mr. Tư was now running a seafood market just a few blocks from the 'Phở' restaurant.

Mr. Hai Sang made no mention of Hoa, Mr. Tư's daughter, and Tuất didn't have the courage to ask - afraid that someone might see too clearly into his heart.

After bidding farewell to Mr. Hai's family, Tuất hurried to the fish market. Spotting Mr. Tư behind the register, he called out from the entrance, "Mr. Tư!"

Startled, Mr. Tư looked up, his eyes widening as he stared at Tuất.

"Is that you, Tuất?" he asked.

"Yes, it's me, Mr. Tư!" Tuất shouted joyfully, rushing forward to embrace him as if reunited with a long-lost father. Moved to tears, Mr. Tư held him tightly.

"We've spoken about you so often," he said. "We never knew what happened. Where have you been all this time?"

Tuất gave a brief account of where he had settled in Canada. Mr. Tư grasped his hands tightly, studying him from head to toe, as if needing to convince himself that the man standing before him was truly Tuất - flesh and bone, not just a memory.

"It's been so long," Mr. Tư said softly. "I never thought we'd end up in the same place one day."

"Yes, this country is so vast," Tuất replied. "Even driving non-stop, it still took me two full days to get here."

"What have you been doing all these years?"

"Well," Tuất began, "I spent some time working in a garage, fixing cars - just like I did with Uncle Bảy. Later, I shifted into air conditioning repair. I've been doing that for several years now."

He deliberately skimmed over the hardships and detours in his journey, quickly steering the conversation elsewhere.

"Speaking of Uncle Bảy… have you heard any news about him?"

Mr. Tư shook his head. "Not a word since those days. I don't even know if he's still alive."

Tuất longed to ask whether Hoa had come to Canada with Mr. Tư, or how she was doing - but he hesitated, unsure of how to bring it up. Instead, he shifted the conversation slightly:

"Earlier, I happened to run into Mr. Hai Sang. He mentioned that you and your wife are working here. Do you have anyone helping you at the store?"

"At first, Hoa helped out with the chores at home," Mr. Tư replied. "After a year or two, she found work elsewhere. Mr. Hai also hired two employees to help us here - otherwise, with our age, it'd be too much to manage on our own."

A quiet joy bloomed in Tuất's chest at the mention of Hoa's name, but he kept his expression carefully composed. Just then, Mr. Tư called toward the back of the shop, summoning Mrs. Tư to come out and see who had arrived. Upon recognizing Tuất, she welcomed him warmly, and together, the couple insisted he come to their home for dinner that evening.

How could Tuất possibly refuse?

The first thing Tuất did was stop by the liquor store to pick up a bottle of "Old Man with a Cane" - Johnnie Walker Scotch whisky, easily recognized by the image of a man holding a cane - as a gift for Mr. Tư. When it came to choosing something for Mrs. Tư and Hoa, however, he thought long and hard but couldn't make up his mind. In the end, following the Canadian custom, he settled on a bouquet of fresh roses.

The Tư family lived in an apartment building that, judging by the air alone, seemed to house many Vietnamese immigrants. The comforting aromas of stewed meat, braised fish, and fried spring rolls hung in the hallway, stirring memories of distant kitchens and familiar meals. Tuất took the elevator up to their floor and knocked on the door.

When it opened, Hoa stood before him. She froze, eyes wide with shock, staring at Tuất. And though he had known he would see her, the suddenness of the moment caught him off guard. His heart pounded wildly, as if trying to escape from his chest. For a brief instant, time seemed to stop. The earth paused in its spin, just long enough for their hearts to catch up with the dreamy years that had passed - before reality gently pulled them back.

"Is that you, Tuất?"

Finally, Hoa spoke, though she still couldn't quite believe her eyes. It turned out Mr. and Mrs. Tư had picked up on Canada's love for surprises - they hadn't told Hoa exactly who was coming for dinner, only that a guest from afar would be joining them.

"How have you been, Hoa?"

Tuất replied with a warm smile, doing his best to contain his emotions.

After years apart, the four of them once again had the chance to sit down for a meal together. The long stretch of separation had only deepened their bond, sweetened by shared memories and longing. Time, in this case, had ripened the fruit of affection between them.

Mr. Tư, once a solitary figure whose only companion was his bottle, now had across from him the very person he had long hoped would become family. After a few sips of 'Old Man with a Cane', he seemed to lose his own cane without noticing. Leaning over to hug his wife, he looked at the young pair with a twinkle in his eye.

"Just let us know when you two plan to get married," he teased.

Tuất noticed something different - Hoa didn't get up and storm away like she used to when her father made similar remarks. This time, she merely looked down shyly, as if waiting for him to speak.

But Tuất was no longer the hesitant man of years past. He answered without pause.

"I know you say that because you care for me, Uncle. But... who knows if Hoa would still have me?"

Being someone with experiences, having worked and enlisted to the far north as a 'miner,' and even having thrived under the reign of Boss C., only then could Tuất come up with such a witty answer to pass the buck to Hoa. But Hoa wasn't one to easily give in.

"What kind of answer was that?" she asked.

The next day, Tuất drove Hoa to visit Stanley Park, a world-famous garden and tourist attraction in Vancouver. There were ponds and lakes, and birds of every kind. Fragrant flower beds invited admiration. Towering pines, cypresses, and hundred-year-old maples stood solemnly in contemplation of time. But instead of wandering through the sights, the two lovebirds chose a quiet spot on the grass, unpacked a basket of cherries, and savored each smooth, juicy fruit at their own pace.

They gazed out at the distant sea, feeling closer than ever.

"What have you been up to since coming here? Tell me," Tuất asked.

"Back in school, during summer breaks, I worked at various clothing factories - doing things like folding clothes," Hoa replied. "After high school, I helped out for a while at Uncle Hai's fish market, just to ease the burden on my parents."

"That must've been tough."

"Not tougher than life in Vietnam. At least here, I could make a little money to help my family. Then I got lucky - a friend who worked at a bank helped me land a job as a teller."

"That's less tiring, but don't you have to stand all day?"

"Standing wasn't the issue. I was more worried about robberies."

"Come on, it's peaceful here. What robberies?"

"You might not hear about them, but they do happen. That's actually why I resigned."

"Really?"

"Yeah. During my six months of training, the bank got robbed - twice. I was terrified. After the second time, I decided I couldn't do it anymore."

Tuất chuckled. 'What a life we've had,' he thought, choosing not to burden Hoa with stories of his own hardships. No need to add to her worries.

Surprised, Hoa gave him a playful scolding. "Are you laughing at me?"

"I'm sorry," he said quickly. "I'm not laughing at you - I'm laughing at how fate plays its tricks on us. Let's just say we've shaken off that bad luck for good. Things will start looking up."

"I thought the same," Hoa replied, "but trouble followed me to the next bank I worked at. I stayed there for a few years. Just last month, we were robbed again. This time, it made the news. Did you see it?"

"I've been so busy with work, I hardly have time to watch the news," Tuất admitted.

"Since then, I've been terrified. I resigned again, and now I'm planning to change careers. I need something safer."

"Maybe it's just bad luck - maybe we ended up in riskier neighborhoods," he offered gently.

"My friends said the same thing," Hoa said. "Maybe I should start looking for a job in a safer area."

Tuất looked at her and, without hesitation, said, "Let me take care of that for you."

Hoa looked at Tuất, touched. There was something endearing, almost instinctive, about the way he spoke, as if protecting someone he deeply cared for. Then, as if struck by a sudden idea, Tuất smiled mysteriously.

"I have a job offer for you," he said. "In Winnipeg."

"You're so strange," Hoa teased. "Who said I'd follow you to Winnipeg? Are you planning to kidnap me?"

"Don't you remember what Mom and Dad said yesterday?"

Hoa blushed, lowering her gaze. Her heart fluttered at how naturally Tuất referred to Mr. and Mrs. Tư as 'Mom and Dad.'

Then Tuất shared the plan that had just taken shape in his mind: he would return to Winnipeg, take over Sister Five's nail salon, then come back to Vancouver for their wedding - and together, they would move back and run the shop as proud co-owners.

"Really?" Hoa murmured.

"I promise I'll try," Tuất said with quiet conviction.

They continued to enjoy each cherry, savoring the sweet, tangy flavor. It tasted like summer itself, refreshing and light, like a reward for the days of waiting, and a celebration of the days ahead.

On the drive home, the radio in Tuất's car crackled to life with a familiar voice from a decade past - Lynn Anderson singing:

'I never promised you a rose garden
Along with the sunshine,
There's gotta be a little rain sometimes...'

Tuất had always liked this song. And in that moment, it said exactly what he had wanted to say to Hoa - but hadn't yet found the words for. He pointed to the radio and smiled softly.

"Those are the words I've been meaning to tell you," he said. "I can't promise you a rose garden, or sunshine all year round."

Hoa nodded, deeply moved. She could feel how much Tuất cared for her - and how he feared she might be disappointed if their dreams didn't unfold exactly as they'd hoped.

Silently, Tuất thanked the radio for lending him the words he couldn't quite say himself. After all the ups and downs he'd faced, he had learned to be cautious with promises.

Then, breaking the gentle quiet that had settled between them, Hoa suddenly asked,

"Oh! I forgot to ask - what brought you to Vancouver in the first place?"

Tuất grinned. "I was actually on my way to visit Little Saigon in California."

However, the next day, Tuất turned back toward Winnipeg.

Love, after all, is the feeling of completeness in the heart. He no longer felt drawn to the glittering appeal of Little Saigon. He was no longer a tourist with a camera, chasing fleeting images of perfection - because the essence of what he sought had already found its place in his heart.

By the grace of the Maker - or, as Hoa often liked to claim with a playful smile, 'thanks to her love' - everything seemed to fall into place for them - from that moment on. Tuất took over the nail salon in Winnipeg, returned to Vancouver for the wedding, and joyfully brought his princess home in a "golden palanquin." And just like that, life began to flow - smoothly, steadily, beautifully - into the past.

There was the joy of welcoming their firstborn, Nghĩa, followed by the arrival of their second child, Nhân. There was the mix of excitement and anxiety in launching their first nail shop, the thrill and growing confidence when they opened Shop No. 2, and finally, the pride of opening Nail Shop No. 3 - just over a week ago - an event that made local headlines and became the talk of the town.

16. Whispering Dreams

Tuất had just emerged from a long, meandering dream - one that had taken him back through memories long buried beneath the surface of daily life. He had hoped to unearth an answer, some clarity in response to the question journalist Ann Blankart had asked during their interview just a few days earlier: "What was the one moment, the turning point, that changed your life?"

At the time, Tuất had chuckled and, in his usual playful manner, considered bringing up the "flashlight incident" - how misplacing a flashlight had somehow set him on the path from village to city. But even before the words formed, he knew it was far too small a cause for such a vast effect. After all, leaving one's hometown was one thing; leaving one's country, perhaps for good, was something else entirely.

And yet, as he looked back now on the long journey he had made, from the muddy banks of his childhood to the snow-covered streets of Winnipeg, Tuất began to see that life was not shaped by a single event. The so-called turning points were often nothing more than pebbles along the roadside. Some caused a stumble, others forced a detour, but all were part of the same road. They passed, as everything does. Life carried on, indifferent but persistent.

What truly stayed with him - what quietly shaped each step - were not the disruptions, but the moments of unexpected kindness. Like a jar of fresh water left by the roadside on a scorching day, placed in front of a stranger's home by someone we never meet. These moments didn't call attention to themselves. They simply appeared - and remained.

Attached to us forever, they were the warmth of childhood, the intimacy of love, the compassion extended to and from others. These, Tuất believed, were what truly mattered.

One such moment lived vividly in both his and Hoa's memory. It was Hoa's first day at a garment factory, where she had been placed by the immigration office. Nervous and unfamiliar with everyone around her, she found herself suddenly surrounded by a few Filipino seamstresses, strangers, each handing her a few coins. One after another. By the end of the day, she held twenty-four dollars in change. That evening, rushing home to tell her mother, Hoa beamed with gratitude. Mrs. Tư, eyes wide, could only repeat:

"People are so kind, my child. You must remember to be grateful."

Tuất rose from his desk and wandered to the window, gazing out at the snowy canvas behind his nail shop. The quiet whiteness beyond the glass seemed to echo the silence of his reflections. Then - 'leng keng, leng keng' - the bell above the door chimed, breaking the stillness.

A customer had arrived.

Tuất turned quickly and stepped into the front room, quietly thankful that one of the nail technicians had just made it in. He greeted the familiar guest with a warm smile - it was the Mayor, now retired, but still a loyal client. He and his wife had been among the very first patrons at Tuất and Hoa's original nail shop, back when the Mayor was still a City Councilor. In those early days, their visits were gestures of community support. Now, as he liked to joke, they were a necessity - his growing belly made it harder for him to tend to his own toenails.

Once the technician had begun serving the Mayor, Tuất returned to the back office to check on the accounts for their three flourishing nail salons.

Moments later, Hoa opened the office door.

"You take care of the shop," she said, grabbing her coat. "I'll take the kids to school. I heard on the radio that classes are open today."

"Drive carefully," Tuất replied, eyes lingering on her. "Watch out for the icy patches."

He watched as Hoa disappeared behind the doors. A tender hush filled the space again. Alone for a brief moment, Tuất found himself quietly reciting a poem he had carried with him for years - lines that spoke not just of a place, but of a lifetime:

Ai về lục tỉnh mà coi,
Nước con sông Hậu tưới đồng An Giang.
Ban đêm đom đóm lập lòe,
Bình minh lố dạng con chim chích chòe khua mỏ hót vang.
Chiều về bên núi Cô Tô,
Thì thầm gởi ráng hoàng hôn mộng vàng.
Hữu tình một chuyến đò ngang,
Trời ban cô vợ đảm đang thiếp chàng.

(Embark on a journey to the Mekong Delta,
Where the Hậu River tends to An Giang's verdant fields.
Fireflies illuminate the night,
Dawn awakens to the melodies of sparrows.
Returning at dusk to Mount Cô Tô,
Whispering dreams to the setting sun.
Falling in love with the maiden across the river,
Heaven graced with the steadfast love of a devoted wife.)

And with that, Tuất smiled to himself. The past had not vanished - it had simply taken root in another land, blooming in quiet, everyday moments. In a snowy city far from An Giang, with jars of fresh water scattered along the way, he had found a life - unexpected, unplanned, but wholly his own.

- End -

AUTHOR

Vinh Quyen Tang, Ph.D., P.Eng..
(Tăng Quyền Vinh)
Ottawa, Canada.

Books published:

1. Bên Kia Bến Đỗ, 2021.
2. Đứa Con An Giang, 2022.
3. Lu nước ngọt, 2023.
4. Nails Tình Thương, 2023.
5. Tứ Quý (Truyện trích từ Bên Kia Bến Đỗ), 2023.
6. The Precious Quartet (Translated from the Vietnamese title 'Tứ Quý'), 2024.
7. Compassionate Nails: A Journey of Love and Resilience (Translated from the Vietnamese title 'Nails Tình Thương'), 2024.
8. Đôi Dòng Sông Nước, 2024.
9. Tales of the River: Journey from the Mekong Delta, (Translated from the Vietnamese title 'Đôi Dòng Sông Nước'), 2024.

10. Freshwater Jar (Translated from the Vietnamese title 'Lu Nước Ngọt'), 2024.

11. Twelve Habours (Translated from the Vietnamese title 'Bên Kia Bến Đỗ'), 2025.

12. The Boy From An Giang (Translated from the Vietnamese title 'Đứa Con An Giang'), 2025.

ISBN 978-1-7773500-8-6